THE FORTUNES OF TEXAS

Follow the lives and loves of a complex family with a rich history and deep ties in the Lone Star State

FORTUNE'S FAMILY SECRETS

With Archibald Fortune's death comes the revelation of a stunning secret: The Emerald Ridge scion had three separate families and one child he'd always longed to find! Can his shocked children come together to find Archibald's missing heir and claim the family inheritance—or will strife tear them apart?

FORTUNE'S FOUND FAMILY

Two best friends pretending to be lovers at a ten-year high school reunion? Sounds like a night of harmless fun for Madeline Fortune, who's still nursing the wounds from her vindictive ex. When things take an unexpected romantic turn with single dad Forrest Porter, though, the wealthy rancher refuses to put their relationship at risk. But sometimes the heart has other plans!

Dear Reader,

Thank you so much for reading *Fortune's Found Family*, a story that was my most challenging to write. Not because of these wonderful characters, but because of a deep personal loss. While writing Forrest and Madeline's story, my father passed away unexpectedly. With his death came indescribable grief. A grief that I was only able to face with the love and support of my husband.

In *Fortune's Found Family*, Forrest's father faced a major health scare, and Forrest was fortunate to have a friend like Madeline by his side. Forrest and Madeline's journey to love resonated with me since I, too, had a second chance at love with someone who was very much a friend. There is a wonderment in discovering that the friend you can talk to, the person you can rely on, can become so much more.

However, there is also an underlying fear that accompanies entering a relationship with a friend. You ask yourself, what if it doesn't work out? Would I lose my friend for life? Forrest grappled with this fear throughout this tale, and it was nice to see him finally allow himself a second chance at love with Madeline.

I really hope you enjoy reading my third continuity in the Fortune series. I would love to hear from you. Please consider joining my mailing list at michellelindorice.com.

Best,

Michelle

FORTUNE'S FOUND FAMILY

MICHELLE LINDO-RICE

THE FORTUNES OF TEXAS

Special thanks and acknowledgment are given to
Michelle Lindo-Rice for her contribution to
The Fortunes of Texas: Fortune's Family Secrets miniseries.

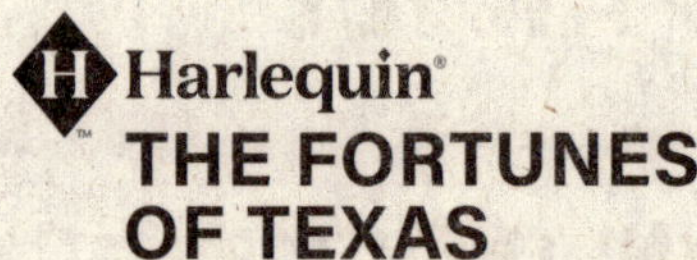

Recycling programs for this product may not exist in your area.

ISBN-13: 978-1-335-14334-1

Fortune's Found Family

Harlequin Enterprises ULC
22 Adelaide St. West, 41st Floor
Toronto, Ontario M5H 4E3, Canada
www.Harlequin.com

HarperCollins Publishers
Macken House, 39/40 Mayor Street Upper,
Dublin 1, D01 C9W8, Ireland
www.HarperCollins.com

Printed in Lithuania

Michelle Lindo-Rice is the author of *The Bookshop Sisterhood*, an Emma Award winner and an RWA Vivian Award finalist. Michelle enjoys reading and crafting fiction across genres. Originally from Jamaica, West Indies, she has earned degrees from New York University; SUNY at Stony Brook; Teachers College, Columbia University; and Argosy University, and has been an educator for over twenty years. She also writes as Zoey Marie Jackson.

Books by Michelle Lindo-Rice

The Fortunes of Texas: Fortune's Hidden Treasures

Fortune on His Doorstep

The Fortunes of Texas: Fortune's Secret Children

A Fortune Thanksgiving

Harlequin Special Edition

The Valentine's Do-Over
A Beauty in the Beast

Seven Brides for Seven Brothers

Rivals at Love Creek
Cinderella's Last Stand
Twenty-Eight Dates
An Alaskan Arrangement

Visit the Author Profile page
at Harlequin.com for more titles.

Dear John, thank you for being my rock, my prayer partner, and at times the one who grounds me here on earth. For Jordan: I wish for you the right friend and lover for life.

Thank you to Adrienne, Gail, Katixa, and others on the Harlequin Special Edition team for your patience with me as I grieved my dad. Your kindness and patience was much appreciated.

Thank you to my agent, Latoya, and my most devoted reader, Sobi.

Chapter One

From the waist upward, her long red hair swept neatly in a bun, her crisp white shirt, black blazer and signature party balloons pinned on her lapel, Madeline Fortune looked the epitome of a successful event planner.

Too bad it was all a farce.

Seated at her oak desk in her home office in her condo in Emerald Ridge, Texas, her ratty cotton shorts and feet stuffed into a pair of scruffy pink slippers depicted the truth. Her business, her name, as well as her professional reputation were in shambles. *No. No*, she scolded herself. That kind of thinking was for yesterday. Today, with two days left in April and the first day of the official restart of her event planning business, under the new name Let's Get the Party Started, she was only going to engage in positive thinking.

After all, Kate Fortune believed in her or she wouldn't have hired her to plan a huge gala celebrating her 100th birthday. The woman had paid her such a significant downpayment that Madeline had been able to put money down on her condo and start up her business. Or rather, *re*start her business. Because after that fiasco in Dallas—Nope. She had promised herself that she wouldn't dwell on the disastrous demise that had led to her swift relocation from Dallas to Emerald Ridge.

There was no point in picking at that scab.

After three months, it was time to let that wound heal. However, that feat proved difficult, given Madeline's faux pas had become a viral sensation and fodder for the internet trolls. *Faux pas?* She scoffed. More like sabotage from a vengeful, hostile ex. Swallowing her bitterness, she drew in a long, deep breath.

Promise. Promise. No thinking about Ethan Flanigan today. Make that ever.

Her phone rang and she hurriedly answered the call, especially once she saw it was her VIP client. "Hello, Kate. How are you?" she asked, squinting at the crude oil painting of her childhood home, back when she had fancied herself becoming an artist. It looked slightly slanted.

"I'm alive," Kate cackled. "I swear that never gets old. When you get to the ripe age of ninety-nine, you learn to appreciate every second."

Madeline laughed. "I'm learning to do that myself. One minute you're up and another..." She let those words hang and cleared her throat. Dang, she sounded sorry for herself, and it wasn't a good look for a party planner to be such a party pooper. She needed to at least sound like rainbows and sunshine even if she didn't feel it. To that end, she had painted her office a light yellow and added a couple of bright office chairs, low-maintenance plants and lemons in a bowl to serve as a centerpiece.

Kate tsked, her voice filled with sympathy. "It will get better, dear. As long as you're breathing and you put in the hard work, benefits are bound to follow. Now, how's my birthday party planning coming along?"

Madeline appreciated that pep talk—she wasn't afraid to put in the time or hours necessary to rebuild her reputation. "You're my only client, so I'm able to give it my full attention," she said lightly.

"Great! I'm hoping that means you have an update for me about Susannah? If she isn't there, then my one hundredth celebration won't be the same." Susannah Simmons was Kate's great-great-grandniece, whom she really wanted to attend her celebration. Madeline had already ventured to the reclusive movie star's lux ranch with her brother, Hayes, but they had had to leave the property to avoid a trespassing fine.

"Actually, I'm still working on that."

"That's alright. I have faith in you. When Archibald suggested I hire you to plan my gala, he assured me that you wouldn't let me down."

Madeline's mouth hung open at Kate's casual name-drop. Kate knew her father? And Archibald Fortune had referred Madeline to Kate? This was the first she had heard about this. She had no idea that her father was the reason she had gotten a job just when she'd desperately needed one.

"Um, Kate, when did all this happen? I didn't even know my father and you were acquaintances. Wait, are we related?" She cleared her throat. "Well, I know we must be in some way since we're Fortunes, but what I meant was, *how* are we related? Are we from the same branch of the family?"

There was a pause for a beat before Kate said, "Suddenly, I'm feeling tired. I'm sorry, dear, but I'd better get going. Talk soon."

Before she could utter another word, the line disconnected. Madeline stared at her phone, knitting her brows. It seems like her ultrarich client wasn't about to volunteer any information. Wracking her brain, Madeline pondered various ways her father and Kate could be connected. But she couldn't think of any.

Neither could her mother, it seemed. Taffy called while she was in deep thought, but all she had to offer was, "Who cares? The old bat saved your neck after that wretched Ethan Flanigan destroyed your business *and* your reputation."

"Ugh. I don't want to hear that man's name," Madeline grunted. "Just thinking of him sours my stomach." Ethan was the ex who'd refused to let go—even after eight months—and when she'd stood her ground, he'd gone after her livelihood.

Madeline had been hired to plan a huge shindig for Congresswoman Nadine Gonzalez. Ethan had sabotaged her event by informing the caterer that the venue and date had changed. In addition, he'd given the caterer an address to an abandoned warehouse. So, when the big day arrived, she'd had no food. Madeline's best friend, Holly Webster, had tried to help by serving appetizers and finger foods, but it was too little, too late. Madeline had lost all her customers after Nadine posted her mortification on social media. She'd ended up losing the second half of her payment. *Plus*, she'd had to pay the caterer who showed up at her office a couple of days after with food, and Madeline couldn't foot the bill. That, too, became fodder for the media. No one mentioned that Holly and Madeline had sent the extra food to a nearby soup kitchen and fed hundreds that day. Instead, she had been mocked for building her business sans the Fortune funds leading to disastrous results. Madeline hadn't used the family money because she wanted her success to be her own and not seen as thriving due to nepotism. She cringed every time she saw the meme with her face and the jeer, How to Lose A Fortune in One Day.

"Stop letting that man affect your equilibrium," Taffy said, piercing into her thoughts. "He isn't worth it. In fact, there isn't a man alive or dead who is. Especially not that lying ingrate who was your father."

Madeline rolled her eyes. "Mom, can we *not* do this now?" It pained her to hear her talk about her father like that.

"Do what?" Taffy barked out, then continued before Madeline could respond. "I for one am happy that sorry excuse of a man is dead. If I was going to be sorry about anything, it would be that that bigamist didn't live to finish out his years behind bars because I for sure would have pressed charges."

Lord, Madeline wished her mother would tone down her rhetoric but that would be like asking the sun to set in the east. She released a long breath and stifled a groan. Not that Taffy didn't have reason to be angry with her father for lying and cheating. But she spewed her anger without thinking of Madeline's feelings. There was no changing Taffy Fortune.

"Technically, he was a *thri*gamist," she muttered, referring to the newly discovered knowledge that Archibald had had two other wives and four other children total. A feat he had managed because of three equally cunning attorneys—and one amazing assistant. While still reeling from the bombshell, Madeline and her newfound siblings had also learned that to inherit his fortune, they had to work together to find a sixth sibling from yet another affair.

From *thirty* years ago.

Ugh. She rubbed her temples—it was just too much. Her stomach hurt from disappointment every time she thought about her father's misdeeds. The only good thing from all of this was that she now had sisters and brothers, something she had always craved as an only child. They had all formed a group chat to communicate as they each grappled with the fact that they had been lied to by the very man who should have been their protector.

Yet, her father had reached out to Kate to help her when her career was at its lowest point. And despite his chronic absences, she *had* been close to her dad before his recent death.

"Archibald was a b—"

And a change in topic was needed. Pronto. "I don't want to be rude, Mom," Madeline interrupted. "But I have Kate's party to plan." She drummed her fingers on the table. "Are you sure you have no idea how we're related to her?"

"Ha! Nope. As far as I know, you're not biologically related, so it must be through some distant Fortune-marriage link. That's the only thing I can think of. Now, enough about that. Let's get to why I called…"

Uh-oh. Madeline knew what this was about.

Sure enough, her mother switched to video call. With a sigh, she prayed for patience as Taffy's face filled the screen. Even though she was fifty-three, her mother looked ten years younger. She exercised regularly and took great care of herself, making sure to keep her blond roots highlighted and styled in a layered bob around her shoulders. Her mom was still in bed and under those luxurious sheets Taffy had transported from Egypt on Archibald's private plane.

Madeline spotted a plate of untouched steak and eggs on her nightstand. A plate she knew would be tossed and Taffy's chef ordered to make another one just because. Madeline would file that under things they argued about when she lived at home but didn't have to anymore.

"Mom, I don't want to be set up on a date," Madeline said, looking into her mother's blue eyes. She was done with men for now after what her ex put her through. "It's mortifying that you think I need help in that area. Between starting up the business and Kate's party, I have my hands full. I'm *choosing* not to date."

"Nonsense. You're hiding. Hiding after what Eth—"

"Mom." She injected steel in her tone. "I'm done talking about this."

Her warning tone didn't deter Taffy one bit. "But you're my only child. How else am I going to get a grandchild? I'm ready to be a doting Glamma or Mimi to some lucky child. Or two."

"Mom, you need to stop watching those *Real Housewives* reality shows. Besides, you'd probably scare off anyone I'd try to date. And seriously, no one told you to make me an only child." A visual image of her four new siblings flashed through her mind as her sense of humor kicked in. "Why don't you reach out to one of your new stepchildren to see if they can accommodate your grandparent dreams?"

Taffy's mouth fell open like a fish, her eyes blinking rapidly. Had she finally rendered her mother speechless? Sadly, she had no such luck.

"I don't want anything to do with any of Archibald's spawn or those two vipers trying to make a claim on his fortune. After all that man put me through, I shouldn't have to share his wealth with anybody."

"Not even me?"

"You know what I meant," Taffy sputtered, toying with her silk chemise. "Why do you always do that? Ruffle my feathers."

Madeline gritted her teeth. It was no less than her mother had done to her and countless others over the years. Just last month, Taffy had called an emergency meeting with the three families to stir up chaos by revealing that Hayes might not be a Fortune because his mother, Damaris, had had an affair. Hayes had been devastated but luckily that all got quashed after he took the DNA test. Yet, now here she was, annoyed with Madeline for messing with her.

"I'm sorry. I just have a lot on my mind."

"Like what?" her mom asked.

"I have to nail this party. It's my comeback."

Taffy relaxed against her headboard. "Did you secure the venue?"

"Yes, but it's a surprise. One that I think Kate is really going to like."

Taffy's eyes flashed. "Tell me. I won't tell a soul."

"Yeah. No. Forgive me, Mom, but you're a flour sifter. You wouldn't be able to resist bragging to everyone you know." Her mother pouted but Madeline wouldn't budge. Luckily an appointment reminder had her jumping to her feet with relief. "Mom, I've got to get going. I'm meeting Forrest in a half hour, and I can't be late." The minute his name left her mouth, Madeline froze.

"Forrest? Who's that?"

"Just a…business associate. A local ranch developer. I'm leasing a piece of land from him for Kate's party that I hope to purchase one day."

Taffy leaned into the camera and arched a brow. "Business associate… *Interesting.*"

Actually, over the past few months, Forrest Porter had become more like a best friend. She had spent lots of time with the single dad and his eighteen-month-old twin girls, Ivy and Violet, often staying over for dinner. But she couldn't tell her mother any of that. Darn her wayward tongue for even bringing the man up!

"What's interesting about a business associate?" she scoffed, hoping her mother didn't hear the light hitch in her voice because even though she'd sworn off men, there was plenty interesting about Forrest that had nothing to do with his wealth and everything to do with his fineness.

"Hmm… What's his last name?" her mother asked. "And why am I just hearing about him?"

The minute Taffy heard the name Porter, and learned Forrest was single, she would salivate and try to set Madeline up. So there was only one response to that question. "I'm not doing this with you now, Mom. It's just business," Madeline emphasized, even as her heart was just a thump-thumping away. "He's going to help me pull off that big surprise I told you I've got planned for Kate. Now I've really got to go…"

Ending the call, Madeline rushed into the master bathroom to freshen up. Her skin looked flushed and her green eyes sparkled. *From anticipation?* Nonsense, she told herself, grabbing a brush and sweeping her stray tendrils before unraveling her bun. Her lustrous waves fell midback and she raked a hand through her curls to give them a gently tousled look. Since Kate was a former cosmetics mogul, she had gifted Madeline with lipsticks and all sorts of makeup perfect for her pale skin tone. Today, she chose a peach tint, applied it, and smacked her lips. She eyed her shorts and gasped. Oh, Lord, she had almost forgotten. Traipsing into her bedroom, she donned jeans, boots and a multicolored striped blouse. Finally satisfied, she slapped on her Stetson and dashed through the door.

A few seconds later, she skittered back inside to grab the cowgirl dolls she had specially ordered for Ivy and Violet. Then with a bang of the door, she was on her way.

Forrest Porter chuckled as his daughters squealed with delight, their pudgy feet racing toward the entrance of the newly constructed toddler playground on his land. The pillars and awning had been designed to resemble a wooden palace, and the entire area was fenced in, featuring a single point of entry and exit. Trailing behind them with the double stroller, Forrest took in the small slides, the huge sandbox, the intricate wooden climbing dome and the baby swings… A smile tugged at his lips as his girls' giggles rang out in the bright, festive space.

Their little feet moved faster than their bodies could keep up. With a squeal, they jumped onto the seesaw. He'd dressed them in leggings, white T-shirts and sneakers. The perfect playground outfit.

"Ivy, Violet, hold on tight!" he called out, rushing to stand watch.

"I am, Daddy," Ivy yelled, her cheeks pink with excitement.

"We not get hurt, Daddy," Violet stated, her knuckles gripping the handle.

When Madeline had pitched the idea to add a children's section adjacent to Kate Fortune's gala, Forrest hadn't been sure if they would get this structure up in time, but after a lot of manpower, her vision was complete and what they had ended up with was a place that was every kid's dream in front of the replica of the Country Cowboy USA. Heck, if he were certain he wouldn't get stuck, he would make his way down the huge caterpillar slide. He couldn't wait for Madeline to see the final product.

Actually, he couldn't wait to see *her*.

Despite the undeniable sparks between them, she had friend-zoned him—and Forrest knew that was the safest place to be after his divorce a year earlier. Besides, he had no intention of pursuing anything more than that. His marriage to his ex, Cora, had been rocky, and then she had engaged in an emotional affair while pregnant, shaking his faith in love and commitment. That kind of betrayal hurt on a soul-deep level. It twisted his gut, especially when she intimated that her affair was a result of his spending more time with his family than with her.

Go figure.

Never mind that Forrest had even arranged for them to take multiple couples retreats, Cora hadn't wanted to leave the girls with his parents. No matter what he'd tried…it had felt there was just no pleasing her, and his parents' home had become a refuge of sorts. Still, he had invited her to tag along but she had straight-up refused. So, when Cora had told him she wanted out of their marriage, Forrest hadn't argued.

In fact, he had been secretly relieved.

Once their divorce was finalized, he'd dedicated his energies to being a good father to his kids. His heart, however, would remain firmly closed to romantic relationships.

Now if only his eyes would stop roaming Madeline's hot body, and his pulse cease its thumping whenever he was in her presence, he would be alright. His physical attraction to her scared him because that echoed how his relationship with Cora had begun. He wasn't about to make that same mistake twice. Not that there was any indication that Madeline viewed him as anything other than a confidant.

She called him her homie, her bro, her pal.

Yep. They were the *bestest* of buds. And he hated every bit of it.

Tired of the seesaw, Ivy and Violet scuttled over to the sandbox, holding hands. Aww. They were so darn cute. He dug into his jeans' pocket and took out his phone to snap a few pictures. That's when he saw Madeline walking up, looking radiant, her long red hair shining in the sun. His mouth went dry. Those long legs and that banging body got him every time. And he was a sucker for a woman in cowboy boots. Forrest bit on his lower lip and stifled a groan.

"Hey, bestie," he croaked out once she was within earshot. His girls were now throwing playground mulch at each other and hadn't spotted Madeline yet.

She crinkled her nose before giving a small wave. It looked like she had a couple of dolls in her other hand. "When I pulled up, I literally lost my breath. Situating the playground next to the Country Cowboy USA was a great idea. The playground is beyond amazing and has exceeded my expectations. The kids are going to have a ball when they see this."

"Yup." He pointed at his girls, who were now sitting and playing with the mulch. He kept an eye out to make sure none made it to their mouths. "Your two youngest critics agree."

Madeline's cheeks flushed. "I admit that they were my motivation for this place."

That knowledge warmed his heart. "Well, I thank you on their behalf. And for placing benches all around the perimeter? *Great call.*"

"I can't take all the credit. I had a good architect who did all this while I focus on the birthday party next month. Based on the guest list acceptance, a lot of Fortunes from all across Texas are planning to attend, so I reserved several blocks of rooms and vacation homes to accommodate the crowd." She looked at him from under her lashes. "My father's other families are planning to come."

"Whoa. How did your mother react to that bit of news?"

"She wasn't happy, but in a way I'm glad it all came out because I hated the fact that he led this whole other secret life that I know nothing about. I also want to know how he and Kate are connected." Madeline then told him of her father's role in securing her Kate Fortune's birthday gig.

"So many secrets," he mused. "I hate them, and no matter how you try to hide them, the truth always surfaces. When I learned about Cora's emotional affair, I was devastated but I'd still rather have all the facts so I could face reality." Forrest could hear the bitterness in his tone. "Even though she continues to deny it, I believe that affair turned physical, which was why she asked for the divorce."

Madeline patted his back in commiseration, and he squeezed her hand. "The man that I've gotten to know is a great friend and a wonderful father. It's *her* loss. She'll regret it."

He smiled. "Thanks for your faith in me. I know I'm flawed but I was committed."

Turning from him, she murmured with a weary sigh, "Who knows why people do the things they do?"

Forrest gave her a playful shove. "Let's quit the doldrums—the past hurt, sure, but it also made me open up to your friendship in a way I normally wouldn't." His lips quirked. "I've probably bent your ear a little too much these past few months...but I appreciate the support." He had been at a low point when he'd met Madeline and she had been such a kind, empathetic friend. Always listening, never judging. When she gazed at him with those sincere green eyes, it made him feel...valued. Cherished even.

Madeline faced him and gave him one of those tender looks that made his heart skip a beat. "I'm blessed to have you, too, Forrest. Thank you for overseeing all this with the playground. I know you're busy with the girls and your job." She shook her head. "I don't know how you manage to be hands-on while running a ranch and acquiring land. I can barely manage to get myself out of bed in the morning."

"Somehow, I doubt that. But I've created a village—a superb assistant, a reliable, highly recommended nanny on call, my parents—they've all been invaluable to me.

Plus, I have—" he tapped her under the chin "—really good friends."

Madeline dipped her head, her lashes touching her cheeks. Great, now he had embarrassed her with his praise. He decided to change the subject. Forrest pointed toward the dolls. "I see you're still intent on spoiling my girls."

"Oh, a girl can never have too much of something she likes." She raked a finger through those luscious locks, her voice breathy.

He arched a brow. "Is that so?"

"Yeah. I spent an hour designing these." Each doll had blue jeans, a plaid shirt and cowgirl boots. Ivy's had pink tones while Violet's had purple. His daughters' favorite colors. It was small details like those that endeared her to him.

She shrugged those slender shoulders before calling out to the girls. Once they spotted her, the twins released loud whoops and raced over to wrap their arms around Madeline's thighs. Bending over, she ruffled their curls before kissing both on their cheeks.

"What's that?" Violet asked, poking her finger into the doll's face.

"This is for you," Madeline said, handing her the doll. Violet beamed like she didn't have at least five more dolls in her play chest at home.

"Mine?" Ivy asked, tugging on Madeline's shirt. A lump formed in his throat, seeing that little chin tucked upward at Madeline with such trust on her face.

"Yes, sweetie. You have one, too."

"Say 'thank you,' girls," Forrest inserted gently, plucking mulch out of their hair.

"Ta you," Ivy and Violet said in unison before hopping around Madeline's legs. Their excitement was infectious, and Forrest and Madeline shared a laugh at their antics. They took them over to the slide and then onto the swings before Junie swung by to get the twins for lunch and then nap time.

Madeline watched as they departed with his nanny. "They are so precious," she whispered, squeezing his arm.

"Thank you." He waved at Junie and threw his girls air kisses as she backed the new minivan out of the parking space before adding, "I honestly can't remember what my life was like before them. Ivy and Violet are the best things to have happened to me in life so far. For sure."

"Wow." Madeline touched her chest. "I don't know if I can say that about *anything*."

"You will. This event is going to catapult your brand to the next level."

"From your lips…" She trailed off, worry evident in her tone. He knew she desperately needed this gala to be a success for her comeback.

Forrest took her hand and continued the well-known cliché with his own rephrasing. "To everyone's ears and eyes."

"Thanks for your faith in me. I'm blessed to have a circle of friends cheering me on. That's why I really want to pay Holly back. Talk about putting your money where your mouth is."

She had confided how Holly had invested her savings into Madeline's relaunch, even coming to work for her full-time. Forrest had been touched by such loyalty. That was a quality he valued with his own staff and friends.

"You will pay her back double," he voiced. "Plus, Kate

is going to be bowled over when she sees how you recreated the Cowboy Country USA amusement park here in Emerald Ridge. I think this was such a creative idea."

She beamed. "Thanks. She loves amusement parks and all things Western, so I figured this would be a nice surprise." Together, they went to check out the rest of the project, which was coming along nicely. It took about an hour to perform their walk-through and consult with the production manager and crew.

Once they were finished, and back in the parking lot, Madeline withdrew her hand to mop her forehead. "This summer promises to be a scorcher if we're a day from May and it already feels like this."

"Yeah, we desperately need some rain, but this is a good day to hit the golf course, if you're interested."

"Nah. I'll leave that to you. Golf is *not* my thing."

Forrest chuckled. He wasn't a great golfer or a huge fan of the sport, but it was a hobby he was trying unsuccessfully to cultivate. Before his children were born, he had fancied himself a rodeo king, participating in many competitions across the state. Cora had made him give up bull riding because she thought it was unsafe, and he'd had no problem with it since his specialty had been tie-down roping and barrel racing. Forrest had been a pro at that, winning numerous titles and awards, many of which were on display in his parents' home. In fact, he still practiced to keep up his skills, but fatherhood took up the bulk of his time.

Madeline's tummy grumbled loudly, jolting him from his thoughts, and she cracked up. "How about we grab lunch instead? Feel like some tacos from Huevos and Tacos?"

"I'll never say no to some carnitas," he said, suggesting one of their favorite lunch spots that had opened a few months prior. It was located just beyond downtown, right at the edge of town, and it was well worth the ride.

Just then his cell phone buzzed. A quick glance at his text messages told him his assistant was reaching out with an update about a piece of land he was trying to acquire. "I've got to take this..."

"Cool. How about you handle your business, and I'll meet you over there?"

"That will work."

After allowing himself the pleasure of watching Madeline get into her truck, Forrest called his assistant. What he heard next had him speeding out of the lot.

Chapter Two

Hay bale fire.

Scary words for any ranch owner.

Luckily, it had been contained, and Forrest had lost only a few hay bales. Even though she had suggested they reschedule lunch for another time, Forrest had refused, saying that fighting the fire had made him hungrier than before—and then he'd texted her his order. His ranch was a good thirty minutes away, so Madeline sipped on water and scrolled through her emails while she waited.

Seeing the reminder about her high school reunion in Houston, she clicked on the message. Madeline had responded to the RSVP, saying she would bring a plus one, at the time thinking her best friend, Holly Webster, would go with her

A flurry of group emails from former classmates expressing their excitement also flooded her inbox. Each one talked about bringing their fiancés and husbands… Madeline was as single as ever. Not that she minded being unattached but she didn't want to show up alone—not when they all knew about her public humiliation. Ugh, she didn't want to see the pity in anybody's eyes.

Or the derision.

Just then, Holly's face flashed across her laptop

screen. She accepted the video call. Judging from the background, Holly was at one of the food vendors that Madeline was considering using for the gala. "How's it going?" she asked.

Plopping something in her mouth, Holly said, "This taste testing is going well. My tummy and my fans thank you for giving me this task and I definitely recommend them for Kate's birthday bash."

Holly had graduated from culinary school at the top of her class and had ventured into catering, which was how they'd first met. Madeline had hired her for an event and they'd bonded because the woman was a true foodie. She was adventurous when it came to trying new dishes, which she posted about regularly on her blog. Holly feasting on crickets had garnered her the highest views, and counting, on her socials.

With that kind of success, she had quit catering to be a food critic of sorts. Holly had a great following and had urged Madeline to use her fame to build a platform. But Madeline wasn't that brave. After the Gonzalez fiasco, she'd retreated from social media and ignored Holly's urgings to start a podcast or TikTok channel about her life after the scandal. *Picking up the Pieces*, though apt, had been the suggested title.

Um no. Just no. Madeline would nurse her wounds in private, thank you very much. And besides, her mother would have a fit if she pursued that, especially since she had refused Taffy's help. Though she valued social media, she wasn't about to get *that* personal.

"That's great. I'll add this vendor to the list and send an offer over soon."

"Perfect." Holly wiped her mouth and gave a thumbs-up. She squinted. “Wait, where are you? I just saw a server go by with what looked like tacos.”

Madeline bit back a chuckle. “Trust you to spot the food. I’m at Huevos and Tacos. Meeting Forrest for lunch.”

“Ah. I heard they have the best omelets and that everything they do is supersized.” Holly wiggled her brows. “And, yay, you’ll be sharing a meal with Forrest. How’s Mr. Dreamy doing by the way?”

“He’s *not* Mr. Dreamy. Stop calling him that,” she said, keeping her tone neutral. “He’s just Forrest.”

“Hmm. Tell that to your face, which is as bright as a hundred-watt bulb. Every time you mention his name, you glow.”

Madeline rolled her eyes. “Will you be serious?” She did her best stern face, hoping her friend would finally drop the usual argument she made every time Forrest’s name came up.

“I never joke about handsome men,” Holly retorted, circling her index finger. “Fine, I’ll move on, since you insist on being a dud and won’t admit how hard you’re crushing on that man.” She cleared her throat. “So. What’s next on the agenda?”

Despite all her success, Madeline knew that Holly was a pastry chef at heart. And that made what Madeline was about to do extra special.

“I have a surprise for you,” she teased, leaning into the camera.

Her friend’s eyes flashed. “Oooh. I love surprises!”

“I know.” Madeline cracked up. Then she drummed her fists on the table. “Check your email.” Then she waited. Seconds later, she heard a screech.

"Stop it! You *didn't*. My eyes must be deceiving me. Please. Please. Please. Tell me this is not a prank."

Her chest puffed. "That trip to Italy is very real and so is the internship with the pastry chef."

"How can you afford this when you're so determined not to use Fortune money?" Holly asked with tears in her eyes.

"Some things, or people, are worth the sacrifice." She repeated the very words Holly had uttered to her when she had given her savings to help Madeline relaunch her business. That money had been used to renovate her storefront, which was almost finished, and she was picking up the keys today.

Her bestie covered her mouth. "I don't know how to thank you," she choked out. "Chef Henri doesn't grant internships anymore. I know because I tried several times to no avail."

"Yeah, well, there are times when being a Fortune has its perks." Turns out Chef Henri loved her father and had served him—and his wives—on different occasions. The chef had sent his condolences upon her father's death. Though she had been grief-stricken at the time, Madeline knew how much Holly admired the world-renowned pastry chef and had reached out to ask for his help.

"But the timing is off. I don't want to leave in the midst of Kate's party planning or your reunion."

"I know but if you don't jump on it now, his schedule is all booked up until next year. Just pack your bags. I'll figure things out on my end. Now, get going, you have a flight to catch."

Holly shrieked. "Yes, I do, and I don't have a thing to wear! I've got to go shopping. I have the best friend in the world!" With a wave, she was gone and the screen went dark.

Madeline cracked up. Her bestie was a fashion diva, with all the closets in her apartment packed with clothes. She had no doubt in her mind that Holly already had the perfect wardrobe for this trip. But who was she to rain on her friend's parade?

The server approached with both orders, and she moved her laptop aside. The Mexican omelet for Forrest and two carnitas in tacos for her—one of which they would probably end up sharing.

Like always.

The smells enticed her nostrils, and her mouth watered. She didn't know if she had the fortitude to wait for him, but it would be rude to start eating. Maybe she could take a small taste, she reasoned, unwrapping her napkin and placing it on her lap.

There was a jangle at the door just as she picked up her fork. Forrest walked in looking rugged, scruffy and… absolutely delicious. He tipped his Stetson at a couple of the guests before sliding into the seat across from her.

"Perfect timing."

She expected him to be covered with soot from the fire or smell of fumes. But she smelled aftershave and ocean and man. And if she wasn't mistaken, he'd changed into a fresh pair of jeans and boots, plus a fitted T-shirt and light vest. Madeline bit into her carnitas to muzzle her groan. The man was too fine for words.

"I stopped at home to get a quick shower," he explained, raking a hand through his coils. Then he reached into his jeans and pulled out a piece of paper. Sliding it toward her, he smirked. "This is another special gift from the girls. I think this is supposed to be a flower and they tried to write your name." Forrest bit into his omelet.

Wiping her mouth, Madeline cleaned her hands and then unfolded the paper to see all kinds of crayon markings and what looked like it could be a letter *M.* At best, it could be labeled abstract art, but it was from the girls, so… "I love it. Thanks for this. I'll add it next to the others on my refrigerator." She was almost out of room there, though.

"Um, you could take a picture before you dispose of them, that's what I do." He lifted his shoulders. "I recycle mine every few months or so."

"Yes, but I can't throw them out. I'm saving everything they give me. I can see their adorable little heads nudging each other as they draw side by side…and it melts my heart. I even have a few of their self-portraits that they colored, with my help, of course."

His brows rose, and he gave her a look that said she was *oh so clueless*. "Er, good luck with that. If I put up every single one of the artworks that they gave me, the house would be wallpapered with papers."

"Whatever." She rolled her eyes and put their masterpiece into her purse. "I'll purchase a keepsake box then." She had also ordered plushies made from the girls' self-portraits and couldn't wait for them to arrive.

He shook his head and retrieved his utensils before cutting another piece of his omelet. "You'll learn. You'll see." He slipped a piece of that sizzling, spicy omelet between those full lips and perfect white teeth. This time, she couldn't mute her groan.

"This is some good food," she said to cover her embarrassment.

A whooshing sound on her laptop signified another email notification. Followed by three more. Madeline muted the sounds.

"Do you need to get that?" he asked.

"Nope. It's probably more of my classmates talking about our ten-year high school reunion."

"A reunion?" He arched a brow. "That sounds fun."

"I guess. I went to this small, private high school, and so I've been included on the email chain about it. From the sound of things, they are pulling out all the stops."

"The event planner in you must be eating this all up."

She raked a hand through her hair. "You would think. But everyone is partnered up, and the thought of showing up solo is mortifying. Normally, I wouldn't care, but after being publicly dragged across all social platforms, I feel my presence there would be gossip fodder."

"Why don't you get Holly to go with you? You two would have a blast."

"My ride or die is going to be in Italy then." Madeline went on to tell him about the surprise trip to Italy she had gifted her friend.

Whoosh! Again.

"Is that another message?"

Madeline nodded. She didn't even bother to read it because she was pretty sure it was more of the same, except this one had added a picture of herself curled into someone's arms.

"Tell you what," Forrest said. "I'll go with you." He reached for the second carnitas and took a bite.

Aww, that was so sweet of him, and indicative of the man she was getting to know

"I wouldn't want you to torture yourself. It's a black-tie affair and it's in Houston."

"But I'd be with you. You make even the most mundane task fun. My girls aren't your only fans."

Her heart became as mushy as the shredded meat in her taco. "You sure know how to fan a girl's ego. What a great compliment."

"I meant it. Or maybe I just want more of your carnitas," he teased, helping himself to yet another bite. She told him he could have the rest because she was stuffed.

"You really wouldn't mind coming with me?" she asked, locking eyes with him.

"Of course, I'll be your date. No one has to know we're not a couple," he whispered.

She secretly wished they were a couple, and that knowledge alarmed her. There were multiple reasons why she didn't need to be paired with anyone—her disastrous previous relationship, her new business, but in addition, a Porter-Fortune connection would attract too much attention, and she already had the fallout from the scandal to deal with.

When Forrest added, "That's a small thing to do for my best bud," his choice of words put her mind at ease… somewhat. Because she was a woman, after all, and wanted to be seen as desirable, as more than a friend, even if she wasn't looking to be anything more.

If that made sense…

He placed a hand on his chin and continued. "Actually, I've acquired a patch of land that I'm scouting for a client who wants to start a ranch in Houston. I just received the zoning compliance, which means I can take a look at the infrastructure while we're there—making our trip dual purpose. You can put those wagging tongues to rest, and I can check out the fencing and grazing area."

That sounded like the perfect plan—she still couldn't believe he'd actually offered to go with her to her high school reunion. But who was she to turn him down?

"Okay, if you're *sure.* You'll be my plus-one." She cocked her head. "Think you'll have a sitter for the girls?" She fretted. Madeline knew his nanny generally had the weekends off, having helped Forrest keeping them entertained plenty of times before.

"I'll see if my nanny is available. I'll double her hourly rate. If not, I'll reach out to Cora. We can switch weekends."

"Well, I guess it's all worked out then." She gave him a warm smile. "It looks like I'll be joining Holly on her shopping spree because I'll need a new dress."

"Awesome. I'll brush up on my dance moves."

His dancing shoes might be staying in his closet for the time being. Junie was attending a wedding and his parents were at a spa retreat, so Cora might be his last chance to go to this reunion with Madeline. Forrest hated disappointing his friend. He stood at the foot of his bed, sorting out his clothes for packing. He figured they would be there for at least two nights and had already taken out his suit to have it dry-cleaned. Hopefully, Cora would be in a good mood. She was dropping by with Ivy's special blanket, which she had finally managed to wash.

Right now, they were in the bathtub, under Madeline's supervision. He suspected his nanny didn't care too much for his ex-wife, because she always made a point of leaving before Cora's arrival. Forrest couldn't blame her. After their divorce, their relationship could best be defined as warm enough—*or cool enough*, depending on how you viewed it. But both agreed they got on much better apart than they did together.

And Cora was a great mom. His daughters were her mini-mes and thrived under her care. Forrest's heart cheered at that.

But he suspected she was also jealous. Ivy and Violet talked about "Maddie" all the time, especially last night during their video call. They had been enamored with those dolls. Forrest had seen her lips twist while on the video call, however, Cora hadn't said anything. But he did invite her over this evening to officially introduce her to Madeline, emphasizing that she was just a friend. He couldn't help but compare this meeting to the first time he had met Cora's second husband, Dean Cotter, in person. Dean had been there to help Cora move out of their home and out of his life.

That had been a distressful, humiliating time. The man preening in and out of his house like he owned the place.

When Cora arrived, they were gathered in the family room where he and Madeline had been playing with the peg puzzles. Physically, his ex-wife was the opposite of Madeline. First, she was short, with thick, dark hair, gray eyes and the olive skin characteristic of most Italians.

Ivy and Violet rushed to hug their mother before returning to cuddle in Madeline's arms, while she helped them fit the pieces.

Of course, Ivy and Violet started pretending that they didn't know which piece went where, so they could get tickled. Whenever they missed a piece, Madeline would say, "Silly, silly," and tickle their tummies. Forrest joined them for a bit, he and Madeline laughing together at the girls' silliness.

For Cora, however, that might have been a bit too much. After he did the introductions, Cora watched them, frowning on the sidelines, her body taut. To her credit, she was polite to Madeline, and even got on the floor in her designer wear and Ferragamo shoes to play with the girls. But right after they put them in bed, she asked to speak with him in private. Madeline was still in his living room, curled up on the couch, watching television.

Cora stomped into the kitchen with him trailing behind, dreading how this conversation would go down. He already knew he wasn't going to like what Cora had to say.

But he didn't expect such venom.

"I don't want my children around that woman and her *mess*," Cora whispered in fury, her eyes flashing. He supposed he should be grateful that she wasn't yelling for Madeline to hear. It was probably because his friend was a Fortune and you couldn't sneeze without the spray hitting a Fortune in Emerald Ridge. That's how many of them there were. Cora was a Realtor, and the Fortunes had brought her good business, so he knew she wouldn't be rude to Madeline. But that wouldn't spare him from bearing the brunt of her wrath. Luckily, he had the brawn to take her on.

"What mess?" he asked, folding his arms defensively across his chest.

"That whole tangled web of lies with her father. I heard all about Archibald and his three wives. He's the talk of Emerald Ridge and I don't want my children subjected to all that."

He cocked his head. "Is this about Violet and Ivy's safety…or are you upset because they get along well with Madeline?"

"Please," she huffed. "*I'm* their mother. I don't have to compete with Madeline for my children's affections."

"Good. I'm glad you know that. So, there's no need to be competitive when it comes to Madeline. No one can take your place."

"Like I said, I'm not worried about that." She gritted her teeth. "But I have a major problem with how cozy you are with *her*." She swung her hand between them. "We never had that rapport."

That sentiment completely caught him off guard. He must not have heard right. Forrest stepped back, his chest tight. "Hang on, come again. Are you seriously asking me this right now?"

"Yes, I am," she shot back, moving into his space. "You and Madeline are all wrapped up with each other. And I don't want her getting in the way of you devoting your time and attention to the girls. They are here for you. Not you *and* her."

"Listen, Cora. You are way out of pocket right now. I'm going to need you to back all the way up out of my business and back into yours." He stopped short of saying, *Out of his house.* "I don't interfere with the girls' relationship with Dean, and you know why? Because I know that you wouldn't have my children around anyone you didn't find trustworthy. And you need to do the same with Madeline."

She jutted her chin. "The situation with Dean is different. He has been there from when they were babies, and he doesn't have all this controversy going on in his family. Plus, if I heard the girls right, you let Madeline ride Samson, and you *never* allowed me to do that. You didn't trust me with your precious horse." She sniffled; her voice riddled with hurt.

So that's what this was about? She *was* jealous. Samson had been with him from a foal and Forrest had trained him for his old rodeo years. The stallion was fierce and possessive and, for some reason, Samson didn't like Cora. He would make a huge fuss whenever his ex came near him.

"Madeline is an accomplished rider. I didn't allow you on Samson because I didn't want you getting hurt. He's picky."

"But he likes her, and you're not denying it…" The silence yawned for a beat. Forrest couldn't refute the truth—his horse loved Madeline. Finally, Cora released a long plume of air and relaxed her shoulders. "Whatever. Dean bought me a gentle mare, so I couldn't care less what Samson thinks of me now." Tossing her shoulder-length hair, she added, "He's buying a pony for the girls this weekend."

"That's great." Forrest kept his tone blasé. He had no problem with Dean and his daughters. His problem with the man was that he had slept with Cora, his then-wife, which made him a chump in Forrest's eyes. "I've already started getting them used to caring for the horses, so they are really comfortable around them." He cleared his throat. "Since you-all are getting a pony this weekend, do you think you want to take the girls with you and I'll keep them the next two weekends in a row?"

She blinked rapidly before her eyes narrowed. "No, this is *your* weekend to have them. I don't want to change their routine."

"Come on, Cora. Be reasonable. They are eighteen months old. They don't even know what time or day it is. It won't make a difference to them."

"Nope. I'm not changing my plans. You've never changed up the schedule before you started hanging with Madeline, so it's clear she's the reason behind all this." She tossed those last words at him like an accusation.

He clenched his jaw. "Again. Not your business."

"Well, you figure it out. This is your weekend with the girls," Cora said, just before stomping out the back door. Seconds later, he heard the tires squeal at her departure. All Forrest could do was shake his head. He hadn't expected her to behave so childishly all because he had a female friend. What would she have done if he and Madeline were actually in a relationship? Unless Cora could tell how attracted he was to Madeline. Maybe she didn't buy his whole they were "just friends" spiel. He dragged a hand through his hair. Not that it mattered either way if she did or didn't. That was the whole point of being divorced—they were both free to move on.

But was he ready to do that? Cora was a definite reminder of the heartbreak that could come from being in a relationship.

He strolled back into the living room and saw that Madeline was right where he had left her on his couch. Forrest chuckled, the tension leaving his body at the sight of her. He had no idea how she folded her long legs so tightly, but she was as cute as the bunny rabbit that kept pilfering his horses' carrots. And, since he was honest with himself, Forrest acknowledged that Madeline looked quite fetching, her bum perched upward and those lustrous curls spread across the arm of his couch. He had a sudden urge to kiss her.

Forrest cleared his throat and she immediately sat up. “Hey. How did everything go with your ex-wife?”

He shrugged. “Not as good as I’d hoped. She wasn’t willing to keep the girls this weekend.”

Madeline’s brows rose. “Hmm… What do you make of that?”

“Frankly, I’m annoyed at her inflexibility, but I’m more upset that I’ll be disappointing you because this means I can’t go with you to the reunion this weekend.”

“You can still come,” Madeline said. “Just bring the girls. The invitation said that children were welcome to attend. Almost everybody is bringing their kids along.”

“But Ivy and Violet are a lot, and I don’t want them overshadowing your reunion. Plus, I’d need you to watch them when I go check out the new piece of land. My team is driving up to do the inspections and I have to meet them there.”

“That’s fine and they won’t *overshadow* the reunion, to use your word. When I looked at the invitation again, I learned there will be sitters and a playroom at the event, so we can have our own adult fun.” Her voice dropped at those words.

Did she mean that? *Adult fun.* Gosh, he would love to have some of that with Madeline. Desire stirred deep in his core as he entertained the vision of stretching out next to her, running his hands through her hair and tasting those full lips…

He quashed those traitorous thoughts—his focus needed to remain on his girls—and plopped next to her on the couch. “That sounds perfect.”

"Yay!" She wiggled her body, her hips jutting his with every move.

Forrest held out a fist. "Here's to loads of fun on our first family trip."

Chapter Three

Our first family trip.

Madeline had spent an inordinate amount of time over the past couple days dissecting that phrase apart. That's why she stood at the edge of her bed zoning out when she needed to meet her cousin for lunch. *Our.* Just that word thrilled her. Forrest could have been talking about himself and his girls, but she would like to think she was included. *First.* As in one of more to come. That warmed her heart. Forrest liked being around her as much as she liked being around him.

Family.

A single word that opened the floodgates to all sorts of emotions. As an only child, Madeline had wished for siblings. Now, she had more than she knew what to do with—and one that still needed to be found. Yet, she wanted a family of her own.

Forrest and his girls were a ready-made family. And each already had a place in her heart, which was why she was loathed to expose them in any way to the scandal. However, Forrest viewed her as a friend.

But…there were times where she had seen a hint of more in his eyes. Maybe this night of fun might be a segue to exploring more than friendship. Like a romance. Her pulse escalated. Was she ready for that possibility?

Madeline wasn't entirely sure. Even though her last relationship didn't end well, she was wildly attracted to Forrest. Her hormone levels got all wacky when he was near and she had stopped counting how much she had fantasized about kissing him.

Maybe it was time to do something about it…?

Boy, Madeline sure was glad she had followed Holly's advice and purchased this smoking-hot blue gown for her class reunion. Forrest would probably freak out in a good way when he saw her in this dress. Or was this wishful thinking? She had also splurged on some lingerie to wear under her gown. Madeline picked up the scrappy, sexy material and dropped it in her bag.

This crush was getting her all twisted up inside. It wouldn't be so bad if she could talk to Forrest about it. But this was one topic that was off limits with him. She didn't want to ruin their good vibes with these pesky emotions. If only her eyes would stop looking and the tingles would stop tingling when he was within three feet of her, everything would be perfect.

Oy, she desperately needed to talk to someone. And who better than her brother, Penn?

Madeline met up with him for lunch at the Emerald Ridge Hotel and poured out all she was feeling.

She really needed his input—from a male perspective—and he was older, a man of experience. Since he'd moved to town a few weeks ago, Madeline had made an effort to get to know him, to draw him out, especially with all the drama surrounding whether his brother, Hayes, was truly Archibald's son.

"If it weren't for this ridiculous infatuation, I would say our friendship is rock-solid. Why can't I be satisfied with that?" she moaned, stabbing her fork into her salad. "I don't get why I'm pining for more all of a sudden..."

"Sometimes, the heart wants what it wants, but if you go with an open mind, you might find that the feeling is reciprocated. After all, Forrest did offer to be your date," Penn said, scooping a large spoonful of his broccoli cheddar soup.

"Yeah, but he was just being nice..."

"No man is *that* nice," Penn muttered. "But what do I know? I intend to avoid any serious relationships."

Madeline sat back into her chair. "I don't know if I want something serious either. I've already told you all about how badly things ended with what's his face. But I wouldn't be opposed to a fling..."

"Well, anything is possible. Just go to the reunion with an open mind. But whatever you do, just don't come back married." Penn laughed. "Because it looks like most of our siblings are getting picked off the market one by one. Love is in the air, and I'm holding my breath, because I'm not swooning over anybody anytime soon."

"Me neither." Madeline drew in a deep breath and they cracked up. All of a sudden, both their cell phones vibrated.

It was Hayes texting their group chat.

I have news from the PI that I hired to investigate Lianna. Meet me at the Coffee Connection in twenty minutes.

"It's a great day outside, and it's only half a mile," she murmured.

Nodding, Penn added their lunch to his tab, and they made their way to the café. Even though it was newly built, the owners had gone with a retro vibe that Madeline really loved. They had tools and knickknacks on display that showcased a love of the sixties. *California Dreamin'* played on the jukebox. Hayes was already there, at the largest booth in the back of the restaurant. Both of her brothers were tall and fit. Penn had blond hair and green eyes like hers, while Hayes had brown hair with blue eyes. Shelby arrived and waved. Madeline watched the tall, regal-looking former beauty queen approach, admiring her chestnut-brown wavy hair. Finally, Jillian entered the establishment. Her long, blond locks were swept up in a bun and she was dressed in a cute, hot-pink cocktail dress. From the corner of her eyes, Madeline could see a couple people snapping pictures and hunched her body to keep them from getting a good pic to post on social media.

For a moment, she had forgotten the fascination the town had with Archibald and his many wives. Of course, seeing all his offspring gathered together in an open space would attract attention. Not to mention her own fiasco with her ex.

"We probably should have met at one of our homes," Shelby chimed in.

Hayes lowered his Stetson over his face. "I refuse to let anyone dictate when and where I spend my time."

"I agree," Penn said, an edge in his voice. "We didn't do anything wrong."

"So, what's going on?" Jillian asked once they had placed their orders. Since Madeline and Penn had already eaten, they requested a couple of waters with lemon.

Hayes gestured for them to huddle close. "It's been

very difficult to find anything on Lianna Dunhill because she changed her name and must have used an ITIN number for any major purchases since leaving Emerald Ridge thirty years ago."

"Wow. So, she really *didn't* want to be found," Shelby mused.

"Yeah." Hayes continued, "But the PI dug harder, using some cryptic dark web skills to glean more information. Turns out Lianna, who used the name Lora Dunn, did have only one child. Her son, Oren was born twenty-nine years ago—"

"So there really is a sixth sibling?" Madeline interrupted.

"Yes. We have a brother," Hayes said.

"And did you find him?" Penn asked, his tone tinged with impatience.

"Hang on. It's coming…" Hayes held up a hand. "Once Oren turned eighteen, it appears as if he cut himself off from everyone and everything. So, we could only confirm his existence until seventeen and there are no death records. So that likely means that Oren vanished into thin air as well, and like his mom, he must have changed his name. Unfortunately, after that, the trail goes cold."

There was a pause for a beat.

"Well, at least we know that there is a child and that he's male," Jillian said with excitement.

"And, we have a name—even if it has likely changed," Shelby added. "We're one step closer to learning the truth."

"What *is* the truth?" Penn demanded bitterly. "That our father betrayed us yet again and he has another child out there with a fourth woman."

Madeline reached over to give his hand a squeeze. "We have to focus our energies on our new sibling, not our father's misdeeds. Oren didn't ask to be here, and he deserves to know who he is. The truth is hard to face, but it must be made known. No more secrets."

Shelby interjected. "I agree. Plus, by us working together to find Oren—or whatever he goes by now—we will get our inheritance."

"Yup. It will be a win-win. But how are we going to find him when we don't have his new name?" Hayes asked.

"I just want to find my brother," Shelby chimed in, patting her baby bump. "Because he's family."

Madeline dabbed at her eyes. "Yeah, I'm getting emotional just thinking about that."

"It sounds like we've all pretty much accepted that Oren is Archibald's child. But we can't jump to that conclusion without concrete proof. The fact is, Lianna Dunhill's son might *not* be Archibald's child. He'll need to take a DNA test to inherit the land by the tracks." Hayes cleared his throat. "After everything I just went through, all I can think about is how nerve-wracking the testing will be for him. Imagine grappling with the bombshell news that you have five siblings—only to then possibly find out that you're not related. We could end up disrupting someone's life for nothing."

"I get what you're saying and I can't begin to even fathom what that would be like and how that would unfold," Shelby replied. "But we do know for sure there is a sixth child, and our father wanted to acknowledge him, so we have to honor that."

"Yeah, there's nothing more important than family," Jillian concurred.

"*And* the fact is that the inheritance could change someone's life for the better," Madeline said.

Hayes nodded. "Well, when you put it that way, I'm even more motivated to find our brother."

A couple of hours before his departure to Houston, Cora texted that she was dropping off a few things for the girls to keep them entertained while on the drive.

Forrest hadn't thought beyond packing the dolls that Madeline had gifted them, food, snacks, and restocking their baby bags, but then his ex-wife pulled up. She had an impressive travel plan that she'd created after watching several YouTube videos. To that end, she had brought him buckle toys and sensory activity books as well as portable potties just in case. Forrest tried to reimburse her, but she waved him off before kissing and hugging the girls like they would be gone for months instead of a couple of days. He hadn't had the heart to tease her since it *was* the twins' first road trip.

Besides, if the situation were reversed, he might be doing the same thing.

Once Forrest settled Ivy and Violet into the back seat, he drove to Madeline's condo. She was at the curb with her weekender and a dress bag. Then they hit the road.

Madeline had packed dried fruit as well as yogurt bites, which they all munched on during the ride while they sang car songs at the top of their lungs. Seeing his daughters laughing and having a good time made the trip a success already.

When they pulled up to their hotel in Houston, Forrest was pleased to learn that Madeline had reserved a three-bedroom suite. By then the girls had tired themselves out, so they went down for a nap within minutes of entering the suite.

"Whew. I'm tuckered out myself," Madeline said, coming to sit next to him on the couch in the living area. "Their energy levels should be bottled so I can take some in small doses."

Forrest chuckled, leaning back. "They keep me on my toes for sure." If he closed his eyes, he knew he would fall asleep. That was until Madeline snuggled next to him—which was unexpected. Her sweet peachy scent teasing his nostrils. Then everything within him awakened and he realized that he was with Madeline in a suite that boasted two king-sized beds, and his girls were not afoot. Peak lovemaking time… *Think of something else. This is your friend. F-R-I-E-N-D, as in you're not going to mess up your friendship, no way, no how.*

Madeline burrowed into his chest. Dang, it had been a while since he'd had a woman wrapped around him like this, and he was loving it.

Neither felt the need for conversation. They could just…be.

Forrest welcomed the quiet. He loved how he and Madeline could hang in companionable silence, and when they spoke, the conversation flowed easily. Nothing ever felt forced.

"What time are you supposed to go look at the property?" Madeline whispered, penetrating his thoughts.

He stretched his legs. "I told them I would be there in about an hour, but I can put it off and ask the crew to come tomorrow morning instead if you want to do something else."

She sat up to face him, her hand splayed across his chest. "Nah, you don't have to change your plans. I was thinking that we could catch a movie later, or maybe take the girls to this indoor adventure park. Or even go bike riding. Whichever one you think the girls would enjoy."

Aww. How could he not be affected by how much Madeline was accepting of his adorable little pieces of baggage? He tapped the bridge of her nose. "Any of those options would appeal to them, but this trip is supposed to be about you."

She locked eyes with him. "No, this trip is about *us*."

Forrest arched a brow and swallowed. See, he could take those words to mean something way different than how she probably intended. Reminding himself that she viewed him just as a pal, he changed gears. "So, tell me about these girls you went to school with..."

"Most were nice, but there were clear cliques, including some mean girls. They were popular and invited me to join their group, but I declined. I have an overbearing mother, and I see how she makes others around her feel small and insignificant, and I knew I didn't want any part of that."

"Wow. I'm impressed at your level of insight at such a young age," he remarked. "Being with the in-crowd was at the top of my list back then."

"And *were* you?"

He nodded. "I played football and almost made it to the pros, but the rodeo called, and I was a goner."

"I searched on YouTube after you told me about your

stint, and I've got to say you were really talented." She shot him a look. "Not to mention really cute."

He pursed his lips to keep the smile at bay. "You think I'm cute?"

She tapped him under the chin. "You *know* you're cute. Stop fishing." The seriousness in her eyes belied her playful tone. Was she into him? Or was he misinterpreting the signals she was throwing his way?

Forrest scooted closer. "Girl, you're heading into unchartered territory here. You'd better back up."

Madeline raked her teeth across her bottom lip and challenged, "I'm not scared, are you?"

Oh, she was *definitely* flirting. The tension thickened between them—the sweet, torturous kind. As much as he was intrigued by where this conversation was leading, he had to get to the property. Forrest placed a finger over her mouth, "I've got to go, but we're going to continue this conversation when I get back." Even as he said those words, warning bells rang in his head. Maybe he should back off a bit. Madeline, however, didn't seem to have any qualms.

"Looking forward to it." She winked.

It was several hours later before Forrest returned to the suite. The property he had acquired needed fencing and the barns required new roofs. So his flipping the land for a profit was on hold until he could address all the necessary repairs. Fortunately, his client was still invested and was happy to wait until it was inhabitable. The entire time that Forrest and his hand-picked team were inspecting the land, all he could think about was Madeline's parting words.

He had sent her a couple of texts to check on her and his daughters, but the situation in front of him had demanded his full attention. He was glad that he and Madeline had planned to stay an extra day in Houston after her event this weekend. He was going to need it.

Forrest had been worried that she might be upset that he hadn't made it back to take the girls to the park, but she had shooed away those concerns, saying tomorrow was another day.

Upon entering the suite, all was quiet, and he didn't bother to turn on any lights. Slipping out of his boots, he padded down the hall to his daughters' bedroom, but all he saw were wrinkled covers, scattered toys and the pillows tossed on the floor. Pillows he had used to barricade them into the bed. Stifling a yawn, Forrest made his way to Madeline's bedroom. The door was slightly ajar and the television was on a kiddie channel.

All three were knocked out. Madeline had a girl tucked under each arm, her hair a halo between them. It was too adorable not to record. Pulling his phone from his jeans' pocket, Forrest took a few photos.

But they weren't the only ones who were wiped.

Forrest's yawn couldn't be contained and his eyes burned. The temptation to crawl into the king-sized bed with them was strong, but he didn't want to alarm Madeline by his presence, especially when she hadn't invited him in.

So he traipsed into his bedroom with extreme reluctance and got into the shower. The spray on his back felt so good that he let the water run longer than usual. Then, wrapping a towel around his waist, he sank onto the mattress. The fabric molded to his body. Lord, this felt so good. He would just lie here for a few minutes and then get dressed.

The next thing he knew, two hands were tapping on his chest—one hand tugging his hair and another prying one of his eyes open.

"Daddy."

"Up, Daddy."

His girls were awake. Maybe if he just lay still, they would go back to bed. There were blackout curtains, and the clock on the nightstand said 5:14 a.m. A couple more hours of sleep would be great.

Opening his eyes a small crack, he scooped them close and made them lie down next to him.

He wasn't sure if he zoned out, but one of the twins now sat on his head with a squishy diaper. The other was sprawled against his chest. Internalizing a groan, Forrest rubbed his five-o'clock shadow before realization hit. He was naked under the covers. The towel must have come loose. He popped up into the bed and felt around the covers. Turning on the lamp, he lifted the blanket to search for that errant towel.

"Daddy..." Ivy whined.

"Water," Violet cried.

"Hang on, girls. Daddy just has to put some clothes on." Ah! It was at the foot of the bed. Shielding himself from four curious eyes, Forrest wrapped himself and slipped from under the covers. Two girls hurriedly followed behind him. Gripping the towel at his waist, he walked over to the chest and snatched a pair of boxer briefs.

"*Daddy, no!*" Ivy cried, clutching the back of his legs.

"I'm not leaving, sweetie," Forrest said, patting the top

of her head, "I'm just putting on some clothes." Of course, now Violet had to start crying, too. She toddled over, tugged at his towel, and lifted her arms. "Up, Daddy."

From behind, he heard a laugh that made him spin around.

"Need a hand?"

Chapter Four

Images of that firm butt remained imprinted in her mind as they worked together to get the girls dressed and fed. This man was utterly irresistible, and Madeline called herself all kinds of names even though she'd had valid reasons for keeping Forrest in the friend zone. Yet she could appreciate that this attraction had been born out of friendship and wasn't solely reliant on the physical. Not that she was complaining about those firm abs, chest and that million-dollar smile.

They decided to take the girls bike riding to an outdoor park near the hotel so Ivy and Violet could run and play under the gorgeous blue Texas skies while they flirted with heated gazes and intentional touches. The sun was radiant and their spirits high.

Forrest had purchased two electric bikes with baby seats, four helmets, and arranged for an early morning assembly and delivery. The man was efficient, which made him even more desirable in her eyes. This man was pushing all her buttons, checking all her boxes, and then some. The bikes arrived just as they finished feeding the girls oatmeal, blueberries and milk. After a quick diaper change, it was time to go.

They buckled the twins in each of the bikes and then

put on their pink helmets. "They look so adorable," Madeline gushed. Ivy and Violet wore matching T-shirts and leggings with light-up sneakers. From the moment they put them on, the girls started jumping.

"Go stand between them so I can take your picture," he told her.

Nodding, she held up the peace sign and posed with the girls and then traded with Forrest to take pictures.

"Let's goooo…" Ivy said, shimmying from side to side. Madeline gripped the bike, though it was pretty stable.

"Goooo…" Violet repeated, kicking the seat in front of her.

"Are you sure they'll be all right?" Madeline asked, anxiety lining her stomach. All she could think of was what could go wrong.

"Yes. The bikes are the best there is and there is nothing but praise in the reviews."

"Okay, if you're sure." She moved to get on the bike, then hesitated when another thought occurred. "Do you think the roads in the neighborhood are safe enough?" Now her tummy bubbled; she needed to pop some antacids.

"Stop worrying—we'll be fine." Forrest slipped on their baby backpack, hopped onto the bike and took off with Violet. "Come on! These bikes are fast."

Gathering her courage, she said to Ivy, "Alright, I guess we have no choice."

"Goooo," Ivy said, holding her hat.

Madeline got on the bike and set it in motion, sparing a quick look behind. Forrest was already at the end of the block, waiting for her. He beckoned her forward.

"So far, so good," she whispered, wiping the sweat off her upper lip.

"Go, Maddieeee," Ivy squealed. So she went faster. The wind in her hair and Ivy's laughter prodded her on. This *was* fun. She stretched her legs off the pedals for a bit and zoomed past Forrest.

"Wheee!" she yelled out. Ivy mimicked her. Then Forrest came up next to her and they held hands when they could and rode with the girls behind them, waving at passersby until they were at the playground.

Both girls cried when Madeline and Forrest took them out of the child seats.

"I don't want to," Violet said in a full-blown tantrum.

Ivy stiffened her body in protest. Madeline felt her eyes go wide. The girls were usually so well behaved, and she was out of her depth. Fortunately, Forrest was there to take charge. He headed to the bench, both girls tucked under his arms. All she saw was flailing legs. Curious onlookers were shaking their heads as the girls were now screaming at the top of their lungs. Madeline gave them the evil eye that said, *Mind your business*, before following after Forrest.

"Ivy, Violet, you both need to stop now or you'll be in time-out," Forrest said in a low, firm voice. Both girls kept crying.

Frantic, Madeline dug into the bag for their water bottles. "Maybe they're thirsty."

Forrest held up a hand and gave her a brief smile that reassured her, then he returned his attention to his girls. "Do you both want to go into time-out?" He remained calm, which was impressive. The girls stopped mid-cry and shook their heads. "Okay, so stop crying. We will go back on the bikes when we ride home. Do you want water, or do you want to play for a little while?"

Ivy sniffled. "Water."

Violet hiccupped. "Play."

Madeline snorted before covering her mouth.

"You both get a sip of water first," Forrest said in a much lighter tone. Both girls nodded. "But first, you both need to say sorry for not listening to Daddy and for making all this noise in the park."

"Sorry, Daddy," they mumbled in unison.

"I accept your apologies." Then he held out his hands. "Come here." They jumped into his arms, and he gave them tight hugs and kisses. Madeline took out some baby wipes and cleaned their hands and faces, then they had some water. Ivy and Violet were now back to themselves again. They got their water and dashed off in the direction of the slide.

To Madeline, Forrest was now a candidate for Father of the Year. "Amazing," she whispered, wiping her forehead. "I would have had a meltdown if I were watching them on my own and this happened." They walked over to the slide to meet the girls at the bottom.

"You would have handled it," he said with an abundance of faith in his voice. "But now you know what to do when it happens."

Not if, but when. She gave a jerky nod. "I'll do my best."

Forrest chuckled. "Don't let them see you sweat." He wrapped an arm around her from behind and drew her close.

"We never finished our conversation yesterday."

Her breath hitched. "That's right. I'll get right to it. I

wouldn't be opposed to an occasional added benefit to this friendship."

He paused. "Spell it out for me, so there's no misunderstanding. Are you suggesting a fling?"

"Yes, that's exactly what I'm suggesting."

Squeezing her arms, he trailed light kisses on her neck, which caught her off guard. She sucked in a breath. "I'd say I love that idea."

This man was not shy about expressing his emotions. He released her when the girls came into view. Her face had to be red. There were a couple of other parents at the other end of the park watching them closely. The girls darted back to enter the slide again.

Forrest wrapped her in a bear hug. "In case it's not obvious, my love language is physical touch."

"I'm seeing that," she said, as they locked eyes. "That's my number two. My number one is quality time."

Sidling close again, he whispered in her ear, "I look forward to getting to know you. Every aspect of you…"

Gosh, this man was turning her into putty on the playground. She touched her cheeks. What would he be like in the bedroom? Her heart galloped, and her breath hitched. She was both scared and excited at the same time.

"How am I supposed to act normal after what you just said?" she asked, her insides tingling.

The girls came down the slide once more.

With a chuckle, Forrest ran over to take his children to the kiddie swings. Madeline took a moment to take pictures of the mountain climb. She might be able to add one like it on her own playground, plus now she could write off this trip as a business expense.

Madeline approached Forrest and began pushing one

of the girls in the swings. "I know you have to head over to the land again, but once you're back, maybe we can have some time to ourselves."

"How?" He pointed at Ivy and Violet. "We have the girls, and I'm not hiring a random babysitter. Junie came highly recommended with an extensive background check."

"I can be creative—once they are asleep."

His lips quirked. "I like the way you think."

Standing by the edge of his new property, Forrest wasn't concerned with the high-grown grass or the problem with the grazing area they had discovered an hour later. Instead, he munched on roasted peanuts, his eyes focused on the temperamental animal by the edge of the broken fence, as he debated that question.

This mare was striking and fiery, with a luxurious red mane. Just like Madeline's. There was no way he was going to let this wild beauty slip out of his grasp. Imagine his surprise when they'd found this thoroughbred wandering by the small brook at the far end of his property. A phone call revealed that the former owner had left her there because she'd refused to leave.

Frustrated, she had told Forrest to name his price. Said the horse was more trouble than it was worth and she was going to sell it to a couple who hadn't shown up, but she needed that horse off her hands right now.

But Forrest knew horses, and this one was priceless. The kind that chose its owner, not the other way around. He had a feeling that Temperance—the irony of the mare's name—would choose Madeline. And vice versa.

Just then, the horse locked eyes on him, kicked her

legs and snorted before turning away from him with apparent disgust. *That's it.* He wasn't leaving without her. The more he watched her, the more he loved the horse. He tossed the peanut shells and wiped his hands on his jeans. Then he called out to one of his best ranch hands, "Go get her, Whitt. Let's take her home."

"You got it," the older rancher said, saddle in hand. Years prior, Whitt had been a future rodeo star, but his jealousy made him sabotage an opponent. He was caught, convicted, and served his time. Whitt had begged Forrest to give him a second chance, and he had never regretted doing so.

Forrest couldn't wait to see Madeline's reaction. He captured videos and snapped photographs of Temperance to show her. It was 10:00 p.m. when he returned to their suite.

Forrest opened the door as quietly as he could, not wanting to wake the girls.

"Hey. How did everything go?" Madeline asked, covering a yawn.

"It went better than expected. Have I got something to show you." He tapped on the pictures and showed her the mare.

Madeline held the phone in her line of vision and whistled. "What a beauty. She's feisty. I like that."

"Good. I'm relieved to hear that, because she's yours."

Her brows furrowed as she returned his phone. "Mine?"

"Yep."

Madeline's eyes grew huge. "Wait. Did you buy me a horse?"

"Yeah." He tensed, "I know it was probably a bit much, but I looked at her and thought of you."

With a squeal, Madeline jumped in his arms, just the way his daughters would.

"Thank you. Thank you. This is the best gift ever." She plastered his face with tiny kisses until they both dissolved into laughter.

Suddenly their laughter faded. A new kind of awareness set in.

Madeline stopped midlaugh, drew in a tiny wisp of air and then made the most endearing sound. Forrest lowered her slowly, her body sliding against his until they stood flush—chest to chest, hip to hip, hands joined. In that moment, they stood soaking each other in and just breathed.

Keeping his eyes on hers, as if asking her permission, Forrest kissed the back of her hand and the inside of her palm.

She nodded, breath catching. Then she got on her tiptoes and gripped the back of his head. "I can't wait to—"

A wail from the twins' bedroom stopped her midsentence. He touched her lips. "Hold that thought. I just have to tuck them back into bed." But there was another wail. And then another voice joined in with urgency. Madeline was right by his side.

"Daddyyyy!"

He broke into a light jog.

"They know you're home," Madeline said. Forrest hoped that's all it was. But as soon as he passed the threshold, he knew it was way more. They were both clutching their stomachs as the tears streamed down their faces.

"You didn't happen to give them a lot of dairy, did you?"

"Daddyyy," Ivy cried, holding out her hands. Forrest picked her up to hush her while Madeline scooped up Violet in her arms.

"Er. We had ice cream and pizza earlier today." She patted Violet's back. "Are they lactose intolerant?"

"No, but I've noticed that if they have a lot of dairy, they sometimes get tummy aches at night." Thank goodness they hadn't thrown up or had a blowout.

"I'm sorry. I didn't know that."

Ivy rested her head on his shoulder and sniffled. "It's okay. I don't think it's that bad. Probably cramps. I have some Mylicon in my bag. We'll give them some to settle them so they can get restful sleep."

"I'm so sorry," Madeline whispered, steadily rocking Violet. "I hate seeing them in pain."

"No need to apologize. Their cries are mostly because they are scared, and they are in a strange place." He dug the medicine out of the pocket of the baby bag on the chest and gave each of his daughters a dose. They both licked their lips, enjoying the taste of grape.

Madeline released a long plume of air. Ivy was now playing with his chin while Violet's hands were in Madeline's hair.

Walking back to the bed, Forrest attempted to put Ivy down. Madeline mimicked his moves.

"No!" Violet grabbed onto Madeline's shirt. Ivy, in turn, snaked her arms around his neck and shook her head. Caving, Forrest slipped under the covers, Ivy still clinging to his chest. Madeline joined him under the covers.

Shifting his head toward her, Forrest gave her a soft smile. "It looks like our night has been postponed."

"Nah, we're in bed together. I'd call it a success," Madeline said.

He chuckled. "How do you do that?"

"What?"

"How do you make me laugh whenever I'm in your presence?"

She shrugged. "I don't know. I'm not even trying to be funny. When I'm with you, you make me happy. Our interactions feel…"

"*Natural*," they said in unison.

Smiling, their hands crept toward each other and then intertwined. Stretched out next to Madeline and his girls in this bed, contentment flooded his chest. And when he looked into Madeline's warm, green eyes, all he could think was that he hadn't experienced such a sense of rightness before. He swallowed. "You're right. This is a successful night and I wouldn't want it to go any other way."

Chapter Five

The venue for the reunion was an elegant glass-enclosed lobby that had a state-of-the-art sound system and a stunning view of the city of Houston. The decorations consisted of blue and gray, balloons and linen, her old school colors. The centerpieces were ornate floral arrangements and there were photos of all of her graduating class.

Smoothing her ankle-length blue cocktail dress with a high slit up the leg, Madeline led Forrest and the girls to her class picture. She had a huge smile on her face and she had cut her hair to rest just below her cheekbone. "I'd finally gotten my braces removed," she explained to Forrest. "And I was cheesing so hard my jaw hurt."

"You were a beauty," he observed, fussing with his tie. He had chosen to wear a crisp white shirt and a black suit, which molded his body, showing off that fabulous physique. But his eyes on hers made her feel like she was the only woman in the room. "And tonight, you're a vision. There's not a man in the room who will be able to keep his eyes off you."

"Thanks," she whispered, unsure how to respond to his compliment.

Ivy tilted her head back and pointed. "That you."

"I see you," Violet chimed in, also pointing.

"Yes, that is me." She smiled, bending over to fix the flower on the bodice of Violet's dress. Madeline had purchased light green tulle gowns from the Lone Star Little Ones. Flora Rodriguez had recommended the dresses, which featured cap sleeves, a tiered skirt and floral appliqués on the waistline. Madeline had ordered them from the website and had them over-nighted to her condo. She had been pleased with how well the A-line dresses fit, which went well with their socks and dress shoes she'd had Forrest bring from their closets.

Thank goodness, the girls had gotten up this morning, pain-free and back to their normal selves. Madeline had been awakened by the light rocking of the mattress from the girls jumping and counting. Forrest was on the other side of the bed, drawing z's. The toddler in her had decided to join them, bouncing high on the bed until Forrest cracked open his eyes. Of course, his good humor kicked in, and somehow the bed survived four jumpers. And that had been the start of a fun, relaxing day watching movies and playing games until it was time to get dressed. Even that had been entertaining—doing the girls' hair and laughing while they tried to put on some of her makeup.

From the corner of her eye, she could see three women approaching, and her body tensed. Earlier, when she was getting dressed, Forrest had helped with the hook and zipper in the back of her dress, planting kisses along the arch of her neck and whispering all kinds of adjectives for *beautiful* that boosted her confidence.

Now, it was that confidence helping her face the vipers who had teased her mercilessly in high school after she refused to join them in terrorizing the other girls in their class. Ignoring their stares, she walked past the women and headed with Forrest toward the elevators. The conference rooms on the upper level had been customized into mini childcare centers. They stepped into the elevator to drop off the girls. Just as they exited, Madeline heard a voice that chilled her gut.

"Madeline? Is that you?" Kathleen cooed, giving her the once-over. She had two women with her—two women Madeline didn't relish seeing.

"Yes, it's me. In the flesh," she breathed out, unable to get around the circling hyenas. Forrest reached over to take her hand. She was about to politely introduce Forrest and the girls, but they didn't even give her the chance before going into attack mode.

"You look gorgeous, considering all the scandal attached to your name these past months," Kathleen gushed. Madeline dipped her head. Only Kathleen would give a compliment in an accusatory tone. The snotty woman side-eyed the other girls. This was their cue to chime in, just like old times.

Ivy and Violet played tag, running around them and laughing.

"I didn't think you would show your face after what your father did," Giselle said, resting a hand across her ample breasts. A move meant to solicit Forrest's interest. Ten years and these women had *not* changed. She eyed them in their overdone makeup and over-the-top designer dresses and realized none of these women had matured with time. In fact, they had only gotten meaner.

"Yeah, I can't imagine learning that he had three wives and three families. You must have felt so betrayed." Bronwyn shook her head. "I mean if I were in your shoes, I'd be horrified."

The women held their hands over their mouths and tittered. Madeline's shoulders slumped as their barbs punctured her good spirits. She could see now that coming to this reunion had been a big mistake.

"So, do you intend to introduce us to your adorable family?" Giselle asked, managing to sound sweet and condescending at the same time.

Forrest had fire in his eyes. She gave him a beseeching look and began, "Ladies, this is Forrest Porter—"

"Porter of the *famed billionaire* Porters?" Kathleen interrupted, practically salivating at his nod. She sidled into Forrest's personal space in a way that Madeline had to release her grip on his hand. Then Kathleen gave him the once-over.

"Yes, that Porter." Forrest's nose scrunched like he smelled rotten fish. He didn't even bother to hide the disdain in his voice. Backing up, he reached to take his daughters' hands. A protective move.

"Your little girls are simply precious, Madeline," Bronwyn cooed, giving the twins air kisses. That got Ivy and Violet giggling.

"No, these aren't—"

Forrest squeezed her arm and snatched her close. "Madeline is just the best wife and mother a man could ask for."

"Wi—?" Her *husband* cut her off with a warning glance. She forced her lips into a smile. "My husband exaggerates."

"I'm sure." Kathleen placed a hand on her chest, but pure venom flashed across her face.

"Who wants a lollipop?" Bronwyn asked in a high, whiny voice. Tugging out of their father's hold, Ivy and

Violet said, "Meee!!" Bronwyn gave them candy without asking Forrest if that was okay. The gall. Madeline's chest heaved. Now the girls were going to be sugared up and hard to settle for bed.

"Where are your husbands?" she asked, trying to shift the conversation into a safer topic.

All three women avoided her eyes. "They're about," Bronwyn finally said, twisting her lips. "I honestly don't care where he is and what he does, really as long as my bank account stays fat." The slight pain in her voice told the truth. She was miserable. They *all* were, and they clearly relished dragging others down to join them in their misery.

Giselle licked her lips and gave Forrest her full attention again. "If I may…your family is blessed with some amazing genes." Then she looked at Madeline and smirked, "No disrespect intended."

Jealousy fired a match, and Madeline's temper boiled. She was not the same timid girl from ten years ago, and she wasn't about to let that rude behavior slide. "The fact that you have to say *no disrespect intended* tells me that you know that you're being trifling right now."

"Whoa. You know that's how Giselle is. It's not that serious," Kathleen scoffed, flipping her hair.

These women were beyond pretentious. Envy poured from them like sap from a tree.

"I think it's best for us to get going," Forrest said, placing a gentle hand on her arm. His touch calmed her, grounded her. She drew in a deep breath and reminded herself that this was a classy affair.

"Yes, indeed…we should." She bid the women a frosty goodbye, and then she and Forrest walked off. She could still feel their eyes on her and knew that by the time they returned downstairs, the news would spread about her being married to a billionaire. She told Forrest as much once they dropped off the girls.

"I hope so. I just wanted to shut them up," Forrest growled.

"I get it—they do incite strong emotions. But I feel guilty lying about Ivy and Violet. They have a mother who is very involved in their lives." That knowledge made the lie feel worse.

His cell phone rang, and he glanced at it before sending the call to voicemail. "I'll call him back."

"Go ahead and take it," Madeline urged.

"No. No. It's all good. Tonight is all about you." A look of guilt flittered across his face, and Madeline wondered what that call was about, but then Forrest gave her a wide grin. "Let's just enjoy the night. Live the fantasy of being the couple everyone wishes to be. Tomorrow we'll go back to our regular, boring lives."

Madeline nodded, but a hollow feeling of disappointment crawled up her spine. She didn't want this weekend to end—or to go back to being *just friends*. She wanted to throw caution to the wind and make this fantasy come true. But it appeared this fleeting moment was all Forrest was prepared to offer.

However, instead of letting that knowledge get her down, Madeline decided to enjoy the evening. For one thing, the deejay was doing his thing, and, for another, Forrest was a really good dancer. He gave her a wide smile and undulated his hips in perfect rhythm to the beat. Then he crooked his fingers at her. "Come on, girl, it's time to shake your tail feathers. Show these people the meaning of *unbothered*."

And that they did.

They danced together, waved at people, made small talk and nibbled on appetizers—neither was too excited to eat the entrée, which wasn't quality steak. But for ninety-five percent of the night, Madeline and Forrest cut it up on the ballroom floor, until the deejay announced the last dance, urging the crowd to grab their loved ones close.

Giving Forrest a shy glance, Madeline allowed herself to be pulled into his embrace. She snaked her arms around his waist before trailing up his back. Forrest rested his hands just above her hips. There was a light tingle where his hands touched. Her breath quickened.

"Thanks for coming with me tonight. I had fun," she said softly.

"Me, too." He ran his fingers through her hair before caressing her face. "I'm enjoying getting to know this side to you."

She leaned forward. Forrest cupped her head in his hands and planted a tender kiss on her lips.

"My feet are hurting and my mouth is tight from smiling so much, but I can safely say I haven't danced like that in a long time. Correction—make that ever," Madeline said as they tumbled back into the suite a little after midnight, the girls asleep in their arms.

"Girl, you were moving those hips like rent is due tomorrow," he joked.

"Make that an hour," was the quick comeback.

Forrest adjusted Violet on his shoulders to keep her head from bopping while they tiptoed into the girls' room.

His body still remembered the last dance—a slow, sultry waltz—and how great it felt having Madeline in his arms.

He hoped to experience that again and judging from the anticipation in those gorgeous green eyes, he'd say Madeline felt the same.

But first, they had to get the girls out of their fancy dresses and into their PJs without waking them up. Luckily, Ivy and Violet didn't fuss much and nestled into the bed, hugging each other.

Madeline placed a hand on her chest. "Aww, they look so peaceful. Like little angels."

He smiled tenderly. "Sometimes, I just stand and watch them sleep."

"They had a ball tonight."

"Yeah. Kudos to your reunion committee for providing childcare and entertainment for them. That was sheer genius." It had put his mind at ease knowing his daughters were close by. When they had checked in on the girls, they had been having their fun—either in the play area, on the mini dance stage or watching an animated movie. Plus, Ivy and Violet had made a lot of friends. Forrest and Madeline had exchanged numbers with a couple of other parents to keep in touch and to plan playdates.

Madeline yawned. "Thank goodness, we reserved the suite for more than one night. I wouldn't have relished driving home at this hour."

Together, they tucked the girls into bed. Then she excused herself and headed into her bedroom, closing the door with a soft click. Forrest resisted the urge to pout. He got that she was tired, but they could have snuggled or something. Shoot, he was spoiled after the night before when they'd had a sleepover in his daughters' room. He beelined toward his room and eyed the king-sized bed. It looked huge and made him feel lonely.

Maybe it was because he was away from home, but Forrest was now very aware of Madeline. Of her nearness. But maybe she wasn't ready, despite her flirting, and he could respect that.

Forrest exhaled. Oh well. There would be another day. Another time. He tempered his disappointment, undressed and hopped into his private shower. A few minutes later, he plodded out of the bathroom across the plush carpet, silently hoping to see Madeline draped across his bed.

No such luck.

Well, apparently, there was only one thing left to do. Get some sleep and quit feeling sorry for himself.

He slipped on his PJs, tying the drawstring, and plopped into bed, resting his phone on the nightstand to charge. The second he turned onto his side, his cell buzzed. There was only one person who would be texting at this hour. Forrest snatched it up and tapped on the message from Madeline.

I'm ready.

Pumping his fists, Forrest grabbed the baby monitor and dashed out to the room, skidding to a stop outside her room. *Act cool. Act cool.* After a light tap on the door, he entered. To his surprise, she had Dior-scented candles, which filled the air with violet and amber.

Madeline was in the middle of the bed wearing nothing but barely-there underwear. His mouth went dry. "Sorry to keep you waiting. I was getting everything together."

His eyes trailed her curvy body. Those legs, those hips,

those *luscious* breasts. "Girl, you are well worth the wait," he croaked. She lowered her eyes, her cheeks turning crimson. "Don't get all shy after you dressed like that."

She gave him the cutest come-hither smile.

Pulling off his pajama top, Forrest tossed it across the room, then tugged on his drawstring. But because he was so eager, he broke the end of the drawstring, leaving a tangled knot. Gripping the sides, he tried to pull the shorts down, but they sat tight around his waist.

Madeline giggled and covered her mouth with her hand. "Slow down. I'm not going anywhere."

"I'm trying, but I want you so bad right now, I'm a mess." Using his strength, he ripped the string and pulled down his shorts. Of course, his foot wouldn't cooperate. So now he was hopping around, trying to extricate his foot. This was not cool at all. "Daggon it. This is not a good look for me."

Laughing, Madeline slipped out of bed and bent over to help him out of his shorts. Forrest appreciated the sight of the cute derriere curled up in his direction. He stepped out and threw the damaged shorts in the garbage can, unconcerned. He had three more like those at home.

Then he hoisted Madeline in his arms, propping her against his chest, and kissed her with the raw, unbridled hunger of a man who hadn't touched a woman in months. She groaned, her body quivering against him.

Tearing his lips from hers, he trailed kisses on her neck before nibbling on her ear.

"Oh, I can't think..." she whispered.

"Good," he said, continuing his onslaught as he laid her in the center of the bed. "That means I'm doing something right. Don't think...just *feel*." Her eyes were liquid pools, full of warmth and tenderness. A flood of unexpected emotion rushed through him, and he poured everything he had into her. It was perfect. What he needed… what he craved.

Truth be told, Forrest wasn't sure he'd ever have enough of Madeline. Of her essence. And that uncertainty scared him—because this was supposed to be a fling. Another benefit of their friendship. Simply two consensual adults assuaging their needs. This wasn't supposed to feel like a taste of forever. Because the last time he had pledged forever, it only lasted a couple of years and had led to heartbreak. There was no way he could make that mistake again. His heart thumped in his chest.

He wouldn't recover this time. And the worse part was, he couldn't talk to his bestie about it. Not when he had crossed the line of friendship with her and reveled in every minute of it. And would do it again without hesitation.

Forrest shifted, intending to slip from her arms to do some serious thinking, but she scooted closer and engaged in pillow talk. "Thank you for tonight. You made me feel desired. And thank you for standing up for me at the reunion. When I went to the bathroom, all the women were talking about how handsome you were and how nice 'our' daughters were. You rescued me…you were my hero."

Our daughters.

Sudden guilt punched his chest. He was no hero. He had lied about the identity of his children's mother, and that was foul. What if someone had decided to post a caption about them on their socials, and Cora just happened to see it? Even though it was unlikely, it was still a possibility to consider. She would be hurt.

And though she had hurt him, he wasn't trying to retaliate, especially since she was a good mother. *Ugh.* He shouldn't have fibbed like that. And the worst part was that Forrest had included his daughters in his lie. Cora had explicitly stated that she didn't want their children caught up in anything involving Madeline's family scandal, and he had gone against her wishes.

That didn't sit well with him. But Madeline loved his daughters, and she wasn't responsible for Archibald's misdeeds. She was *innocent* and shouldn't be judged for it. That made him feel a little better.

"Forrest? You awake?" Madeline rubbed his arm. Shoot, he had been so caught up in his self-flagellation that he'd forgotten she was waiting for a response.

"Yeah. A lot of unexpected things happened this weekend…" was his vague but honest reply.

Something in his tone must have conveyed his jumbled emotions, because she turned to face him. "Do you have regrets about sleeping with me?" she asked in a small voice.

That snapped him out of his thoughts. He snuggled closer and kissed the top of her head, hoping that gesture would ease her discontent. "No, of course not. Your body was a gift I enjoyed unwrapping. And you know when you get a good gift, you just want to keep touching it, playing with it…" Those words came easily because he spoke his truth. His hands followed his mouth, and his body awakened again.

She sucked in a breath of air. "See, it's because you say and do stuff like that that we ended up here."

Yes, his wayward mouth kept writing checks he couldn't afford to pay. But his mouth, mind, and possibly his heart, had a will of their own when it came to Madeline.

"Do you want me to stop?" he asked, praying she would say yes, desperately hoping she would say no.

"No."

Pushing aside his conflicting emotions, Forrest made love to Madeline again. The second time was even sweeter than before. Madeline fell asleep shortly after that, but Forrest found himself awake.

Unsettled.

Being with her was too right. Too easy. Too…addicting. The whole point of a fling was that it was about having fun with no strings attached. Yet, here he was, full of angst. Uncertainty. Because this woman could break his heart. She had the power to get him all twisted then hang him out to dry. His only saving grace was that she didn't know it. And it was up to him to make sure she never did.

Chapter Six

She was past the point of return.

The brightness of the sun seeped through the blackout curtains. Madeline extended her arms and stretched before patting the space next to her. *Cool.* The clock said 6:08 a.m. Forrest must already be up. She cocked her ears, but it didn't sound like he was in the bathroom, so maybe he had gone to check on the girls.

The man had worn her out, leaving her body aching in the best possible way. She stared up at the ceiling, and exhaled. Last night, she'd found out why the act between a man and woman was called *making love.* Because Forrest had cherished her body like it was a prized trophy. He'd been relentless in his pursuit of giving her pleasure—tender and passionate, a combination that had tripped her crush into something deeper.

Something dangerously close to love.

And that scared her. But she felt safe enough to talk to Forrest about how vulnerable she was feeling. One thing she valued was that she and Forrest had built a solid friendship before becoming lovers.

She showered and dressed in a denim top, white jeans and denim boots, then headed out into the living area.

Forrest and his daughters were asleep on the couch. They all had their mouths open and their brows slightly knitted.

Aww. She took a picture and wondered if her own father had spent nights on the couch with her like this when she was a little girl. Before the bombshell revelations, Madeline would have said yes. But how could Archibald truly spend quality time with her or any of her siblings when he had three families? Hanging around with Forrest had taught her one thing: parenting was a full-time job and, honestly, neither of her parents had been committed like that.

Taffy was too self-absorbed and, at best, her father had been a catch-me-if-you-can, see-you-if-I-see-you kind of dad. He had attempted to bond with her, but his attention had been spread thin, so there were definite gaps.

Gaps that Ivy and Violet wouldn't experience. The twins were fortunate to have a mother and a father dedicated to their well-being. And Madeline treasured being a part of Ivy and Violet's lives.

She considered it an honor that Forrest trusted her with his two precious bundles. Being around the girls brightened her life. Tiptoeing, Madeline left the room and took the elevator down to the four-star restaurant in the lobby to get them breakfast since they hadn't ordered room service.

Lovemaking the night before had her famished, so she ordered a smorgasbord of breakfast items and then left a generous tip to get it all boxed up. There was a queue by the elevator, and she ended up in the back of the car. They stopped on the second floor and more people got in. Madeline didn't think anything of it until she heard a voice she recognized.

Cora?

That was a strange coincidence that Forrest's ex would be at the same hotel. Hadn't she said she was buying the girls a pony this weekend? What was she doing here in Houston?

"I really wish we had gotten that mare. She was gorgeous," Cora was saying to the man next to her, whom Madeline deduced must be her husband, Dean.

"Yes, but someone beat us to it," the gentleman said, rubbing her back. "But we were a day late and a dollar short, as the saying goes."

Madeline got a good look at the man whom Cora had chosen over Forrest. He was tall, lanky and clean-cut with a square jawline. Nothing that stood out. But there was no explaining love and attraction, because from where she stood, there was no competition.

Oh well, Cora's loss was her gain.

"But it's okay. We aren't leaving empty-handed since we were still able to get the girls their pony. So, this weekend wasn't a bust. It was quite a success."

Madeline expected the other woman to contradict or sulk, since Forrest had implied their relationship was rocky, but Cora merely nodded. "You have a good point there. See, that's why I love you. You always see the brighter side," she said, and kissed Dean on the cheek.

Wow.

Cora and Dean exited on the floor below hers without noticing her presence. She heaved a sigh of relief, continuing up to her floor. Scurrying out of the elevator, she couldn't wait to tell Forrest all she had heard. By this time, all three should be up. The girls were probably in the bath or brushing their teeth.

Unlocking the door to the suite, she popped inside and gasped, almost dropping the bag of food. The girls were up. *Oh, were they.* Aghast, she looked around, her mouth falling open. "What the—"

"Hi, Maddie," Violet said, jumping, white liquid oozing from her tightly clutched fists.

Ivy ducked behind the couch, like she knew she had done something wrong.

"You might as well come out. Don't hide now," Madeline said to Ivy. "Your daddy is going to be upset when he sees what you did."

Violet ran over to join her sister and scrunched low. Yep, they knew they were in trouble. *Smart little troublemakers.* Poor things actually believed she couldn't see them, which made her laugh despite the horrific scene before her.

Madeline figured the girls must have gotten into the bathroom. Lord knows what it must look like in there. The empty bottle, the evidence, rested at the edge of the sofa.

A strong scent of jasmine was in the air, and it took a moment for her to place what it was. *Lotion.* Both girls were covered in it from head to toe, right along with the couch. Soils from the lotion covered the microfiber. The couch would most definitely have to be replaced. Forrest was still out cold, his lower body covered in dollops of the substance. Poor guy hadn't even stirred—he must've been completely tuckered out from their all-nighter. She gave herself a mental tap on the back.

Then she took some pictures and turned on the video camera.

"Forrest," she called out, but his only answer was a loud snore. She called his name again, but he didn't even budge. Scanning the area with her phone, Madeline pressed Stop and went over to the kitchen to place the bag in the middle of the counter. Breakfast would have to wait.

Next, she scooped both girls under her arms, very aware that her blouse would never be the same and her jeans would need washing, then rushed to start up the bath.

It was the sound of laughter that woke him up. And since then, Forrest hadn't stopped moving after his initial shock at the sight that greeted him. The couch had permanent oil stains from the lotion, and there were little fingerprints all over the glass coffee table. How could he have slept through this? What kind of parent did that make him? And was the lotion also smeared on his pants?

He jogged down the hall toward the source of the noise to see Madeline sitting by the tub, her back turned away from him, washing Ivy's and Violet's hair. He couldn't imagine how these two adorable girls, giggling and playing in the bathtub, could have wreaked such havoc in the living room.

He had been so tired that he hadn't even noticed when they'd awakened. Cora's warning about him being too devoted to Madeline to give the girls the attention they needed whipped at him. Was she right about that?

Madeline hadn't noticed him as yet, so he leaned by the doorjamb to observe. Forrest was struck by her beauty and how sweet she was with his girls. After a fitful night, he had decided not to mention anything to Cora about what he'd said. Why purposely put his foot into an anthill? No one got hurt, and besides, the girls were too young to understand. Now, if only his conscience would ease as he found himself questioning what was next for him and Madeline.

They had crossed the boundary of friendship, and there was no backtracking. Only he had no idea what moving forward entailed. Forrest couldn't offer her more than a casual affair, and Madeline deserved more than that. Maybe he needed to cool things off a bit between them. The last thing he wanted was to hurt Madeline, but he had never slept so soundly that he didn't hear his daughters wake up. Until now.

And it was because he'd been with Madeline all night.

He wasn't blaming her, of course, because he had been a willing participant. He just didn't want to feel as if he was losing focus on his girls.

"Hey," he called out, stuffing his hands in his pockets. "I'm sorry about all this. I should have heard them get up."

Madeline swung around. There were soap bubbles in her curls and on her cheeks, which was the cutest thing. He had to remind himself that his heart had to remain closed. For both their sakes.

Ivy held on to the tub and tried to stand. "Daddy!"

"Eee!" Violet said, since Madeline was washing her hair.

Madeline gave him a beautiful smile, and the warmth in her eyes made his stomach churn. "Don't apologize. Taking care of Ivy and Violet—" her voice dropped "—and me, has to be exhausting."

"*Exhausting* isn't the word I would use. I love doing things for them. And you." He pointed at his daughters, who were attempting to eat the bubbles. "Need a hand?"

"Nope. You go get cleaned up. I've got this."

Giving her a quick nod, Forrest returned to his room to

shower, tossing his soiled pajamas. Then, donning a shirt and his jeans, he contacted the hotel manager to pay for a replacement sectional and, seeing the cold bag of food, ordered fresh room service.

All this and it wasn't even 8:00 a.m.

Then he checked his voicemail on his cell and gritted his teeth. He had forgotten to call back the engineer. Last night at the reunion, he had sent the call to voicemail because he had been occupied with Madeline's bullies. The words, *Tonight is all about you*, taunted him.

He *was* losing focus. With his children and with his business. A business he had built from scratch without his family's help. It was time to take back the reins, starting now.

Fear propelled him toward the bathroom. Madeline had just opened the drain. The girls looked like prunes, and now her blouse was all wet, giving him a delectable view of the outline of her breasts. Oh, this was *not* going to be easy.

Averting his eyes, Forrest helped get the girls out of the tub and into their bedroom, then urged Madeline to go pack. "I'll take it from here. Thanks."

"Are you sure you don't need my help?"

"Yep. I've done this without assistance plenty of times. Besides, you've done enough." He tried to keep his tone light, but there was no disguising the fact that he was dismissing her.

"Okay..." She paused for a beat, studying him. "Are you sure you're okay?" The girls were bouncing around the room while they spoke.

"Yes, I just have a lot on my mind. I was so caught up with you last night, I missed a call from the engineer.

Sent it to voicemail," he clipped out, aware his words sounded slightly accusatory. "And now there's a major problem with the irrigation I have to deal with before we head back to Emerald Ridge today."

He stalked over to the baby bag, resentment tight in his chest, and took out the matching outfits of shorts and tees for the twins. Forrest dug around for the lotion before he remembered that they had used it all up.

Madeline came over and placed a hand on his arm, brow knitted. "Why does it sound like you're blaming me? I told you to take the call. You chose not to."

"You're right." He dragged a hand through his curls. "It's on me, which is why I plan to fix it."

"Fix it how?" she demanded, challenging him.

Silence reigned between them; the words stuck in his throat.

She sighed. "Never mind. I see you're in a bad mood, so I'll leave you be. I'm here when you want to man up and speak your mind." She gave him a pained look, her eyes glassy, before shaking her head and walking off.

Forrest felt like a heel but it was better that he hurt her now than later. Nah, that thinking was messed up. He shouldn't have hurt her at all, but he had to back off. He was too much into Madeline—the way he had been with Cora—and look how that turned out. *I'm doing the right thing. The right isn't always the easy thing.* He kept those thoughts on repeat, even as he asked himself how on earth he was going to do this. How was he going to put distance between him and the best friend he had ever had?

Chapter Seven

Even with the AC on, Madeline was roasting in the truck while she waited for Forrest. That's because he had parked right in the path of the sun's glare. Her skin heated right along with her anger at him.

Forrest had been gruff and standoffish, which made for a tense ride over to scope out his land. That's why she had opted to stay in the vehicle with the girls, who had fallen asleep. She didn't want to lose her patience or temper with her friend, and so some space between them was best, until he was ready to share what was really going on inside that brain of his.

If she allowed herself to dwell on his stinky attitude, she might snap at him for acting like a jerk after all they had shared last night.

Oh, snap, maybe she had dissatisfied him in bed, which could be why he had withdrawn from her. She hadn't been with many men, but Ethan hadn't had any complaints. Although that could be because Ethan had been content to let her do most of the work. She shoved her ex out of her mind. Thinking about him would just serve to spoil her day before it even began.

Forrest had said he didn't have regrets, but was he just being nice about that? One of the things she valued about him was his honesty, but if the situation were reversed, would she tell him that he sucked in bed?

No. She might gently teach him what she liked…but Forrest was a skillful lover, devoted to her pleasure and ensuring she received ultimate fulfillment. And she had returned the favor. Ugh, she needed a distraction so she could stop obsessing over her sexual prowess.

Reaching for her phone, Madeline pulled up the browser and typed in the search bar, How did Archibald Fortune accumulate his wealth?

While she waited for the results to load, Madeline prayed that her father hadn't been involved in anything nefarious. She and her siblings had recently learned that he had been on his own since fourteen, and that had made her wonder how he'd ended up with so much money. From a couple of articles she'd perused, she'd learned that he had worked as a ranch hand in exchange for room and board. Another article talked about her father inheriting his fortune and then investing in ventures, but she wasn't sure how concrete or reliable that information was.

Abandoning her search, Madeline needed to call Holly. Hopefully, her bestie would be able to talk despite the time difference. She needed to unload.

"Hey, love. How are you?" Holly asked as soon as her face lit up the screen.

Seeing those kind hazel eyes and that wide smile made her tear up. "I would be doing great if my stomach wasn't in knots."

"What's going on?"

It struck her that her friend was overseas, in another country. Madeline needed to make sure Holly was fine before dumping her worries on her. "I can wait." She waved. "Tell me all about how it was meeting Chef Henri."

"It is a dream come true, and I have literally pinched myself to ensure this is all real," Holly shrieked, excitement on her face. "He is every bit as wonderful and as challenging as I thought."

That made her heart warm. "I'm so glad to hear that. I know how you love pushing your limits, so this is a great experience for you. Plus, you sound and look so happy. Italy agrees with you."

"I agree. There's something in the air here that just rejuvenates me. I am learning so much and I'm working on how to incorporate some of what I've learned here into our business."

"I don't know how fancy you can make burgers, hot dogs and the usual finger foods."

"Believe me, I can. It's all about how it's done. The enhancement that makes it *prim'ordine*. Takes it to the *livello successivo*," she said, blending English and Italian words.

"Alright. It's all about the taste, though," Madeline warned.

"For sure." Holly leaned in. "Now, enough about me. Back to you. What's going on?"

Madeline peeked into the back seat to ensure she hadn't awakened the twins. Keeping her voice low, she began, "Forrest and I took our friendship to the next level, and now he's acting aloof, distant, and I don't know how to read these mixed signals. I'm worried about us."

"First, let me squeal," Holly said, clapping her hands and doing a little jig with her shoulders. "I knew it was a matter of time before chemistry won out. It took you both way too long to acknowledge that."

"Yeah, but now I kind of wish we hadn't," Madeline mumbled.

Her bestie held up her index finger. "You didn't let me finish." She held up a second finger. "Second, you have nothing to worry about with your and Forrest's friendship. You two are rock solid. A roll in the sheets can't destroy what you've built."

"Then why is he backing off from me?" Madeline ran through all that had transpired that morning. Especially the part about him not being able to look her in the eyes. "Maybe he's afraid to tell me that I suck at lovemaking," she half joked, even as she remembered making his toes curl.

"Nonsense. I doubt that very much. The dynamics of your friendship changed, that's all. He's probably just processing everything that happened and just needs some time. Unless he tells you that he was dissatisfied, don't jump to that conclusion." Holly cocked her head. "Are *you* disappointed?"

"No. Far from it." She placed a hand on her chest. "Being with Forrest made me acknowledge that I have strong feelings for him. I thought it would be the same for him." Madeline dabbed at her eyes—the realization that it wasn't saddened her heart. She had poor taste when it came to love. Look at how vindictive Ethan had become after claiming to be in love.

She straightened. She *wasn't* going to fall apart.

Holly gave her a look of sympathy. "Aww, friend. Love can be like a seesaw with its ups and downs, but it is worth the ride. The scale might be tipped heavier on your end, but in time, it will balance out. He just needs to catch up."

The wedge in her chest eased. "See, that's why I love you. You always know what to say."

"Just doing what you have done for me countless times. Being a friend. You're the kind of woman to hold on to, and that's why I know you have nothing to worry about when it comes to your relationship with Forrest. You're invaluable and he is too smart a man to let you go."

After those words, she choked out, "You're going to have me boohooing if you don't stop."

Blowing her a kiss, Holly waved. "Talk soon. Keep me posted." Every woman needed a friend like Holly. Her friend was right. She and Forrest had a good thing. Every relationship had conflict but their respect for each other would make this a little easier to navigate.

Forrest returned not too long after. "How did it go with the irrigation issue?" she asked.

"Fine," he muttered, once again not making eye contact. "Still got more to do." He checked on the girls before turning on the ignition. "The weather is good and the roads are clear, so we should be home in no time."

He spoke as if he were forcing the words out, as if he couldn't bear to waste his breath on her. Madeline squared her shoulders. Her chat with Holly had boosted her confidence so, though Forrest was still sulky, she refused to allow his attitude to darken her mood. She was going to talk to him and she knew just what would get him talking.

"Well, that's good. With everything going on, I forgot to tell you that I saw Cora in the elevator."

He swung his head her way. "What? When?"

"Yeah, she got in after me, so she didn't see me," Madeline explained. "But she was yammering on about losing out on a mare with her husband."

For some reason, he bunched his lips, gripped the wheel and didn't say another word the entire ride home.

That licked the flames of her anger. Well, if he wanted to freeze her out, then she would be a glacier. When he pulled up to her curb, she jumped out, grabbed her weekender, bid him a frosty goodbye and came just short of slamming the door.

Because of the girls.

Ivy and Violet were waving, blowing her air kisses and giving her the sweetest goodbyes. And even though her heart broke, she found the strength to give them her most cheerful smile.

He'd had a sinking feeling that the horse he had bought for Madeline was the same one Cora and Dean had wanted to buy. That was all he could think about as he drove home. Cora could have been talking about another mare, but the fact that she had stayed at the nearest hotel to his land could not have been a coincidence. When Madeline mentioned it, goose bumps had popped up on his flesh. But to be sure, Forrest had called the previous owner, and she confirmed the prospective buyer's name as Cotter.

It was a good thing that Junie was back from the wedding and able to tend to the twins because he was in a daze. Forrest walked down to his stable and had his ranch hands saddle up Samson.

"I'm so glad you're here," the young girl said. "He's in a mood and could use the exercise. I think it's because of that new mare next to his stall. She's been kicking up a fuss all morning. Whitt is going to let her out for a bit—he's the only one she trusts so far."

Forrest took a peek at the mare. God, she was a beauty, albeit furious at being caged. He chuckled. "That sounds like a good idea. Temperance would be a good match for Samson. They'll be friends in no time." Just like he and Madeline.

His gut clenched.

Suddenly, he wished he could call her so they could ride together. But he was probably the last person she wanted to hear from right now. Forrest blew out a long breath, mounted his horse, and started with a trot. Once they hit the open field, Samson broke into a gallop, and Forrest returned to his thoughts.

Cora would be furious if she learned he had been the purchaser. Somehow, she would accuse him of doing it on purpose. Not that he generally cared—that was the point of being divorced. But just the night before, he had lied about the identity of the mother of his twins.

Should he tell Cora what he had done at the reunion?

Guilt covered him in waves, and he ended his ride early. Samson wasn't happy about it. However, Forrest needed more than a ride to clear his head. He decided to talk to Trevor and Jonathan. They had formed a great bond over ranching, horses and relationships, and hopefully his cousins would give him the clarity he needed.

Should he give Cora the horse? But how could he, when he had already surprised Madeline with the mare? And Cora would question him relentlessly about why he was giving her a horse—and so would Dean. Nope, it was best he left things be, especially since Madeline had been elated at the gift.

She hadn't even ridden Temperance yet. Not that she would be in a hurry to, given his attitude. He massaged his temples before calling his cousins. Both were very vocal and quick with their responses once he had explained everything.

"First, let go of all that guilt. Your intentions were honorable, so you need to shift gears. Last night was about Madeline. Madeline, *not* Cora," Jonathan emphasized.

"What kills me is that Cora wasn't worried about you when she was all wrapped up with Dean. So, I don't know why you're stressing about that woman," Trevor said.

Forrest nodded, though that memory pinched a little.

"See, that's the difference between you and her, bro. You have a conscience. She doesn't. Cora clearly doesn't feel an ounce of guilt putting demands on you not to let Madeline interfere with you being a good dad to your daughters, especially after she blew up her whole family because of a man," Trevor continued.

"Dang. I didn't see it that way." His boys were making sense. The tightness in his gut loosened.

"Yeah, anybody who knows you knows you are dedicated to your girls. So you shouldn't even entertain that nonsense. Now, let's talk about the woman who's got you all teeheeing with happiness," Trevor added.

"I don't know about teeheeing." He patted his shoulders. "I've got to keep my man card intact. But I've never laughed and joked with anyone the way I do with Madeline. She gets me in ways I can't imagine."

Jonathan gave him a pointed stare. "Yet despite how great she is, you gave her the cold shoulder, dude, right after making love to her." He shook his head. "She didn't deserve that."

"Yeah, I've to agree that was foul. It was what I would call rank behavior," Trevor added.

Forrest crossed his hands over his face. “You guys are coming at me hard but I guess I had it coming.”

“You think?” Jonathan scoffed.

“It’s because we got nothing but love for you that we have to tell you straight up when you’re being doggish.”

“Yeah. I know and I appreciate you guys so much for being my sounding board.” Forrest rubbed between his eyes. “I know I’ve got to mend things with Madeline and preserve our friendship. And, yes, I owe her an apology, big-time. Our night together was incredible…and that left me shaking in my boots. But even though our connection is off the charts, all I can think about is getting hurt again. Look what happened the last time I opened my heart.”

“Well, I’m proof that there is the right person for you,” Jonathan said. “But, cuz, you have to trust your judgment. Do what is going to work for you.”

“I’m a witness as well,” Trevor said. “You can have both.”

“I do get what you both have,” Forrest admitted. “However, that’s not in the cards for me. You both are so stinking happy, it’s nauseating.”

“Jealous much?” Jonathan teased. “Stop being a punk and give yourself the chance to find out if Madeline is the one.” He smirked. “That’s if she will talk to you.”

“I might not be her favorite person, but I don’t think she would shut the girls out or neglect the horse I bought her.”

Trevor shook his head. “*Horse?* Hold up. You didn’t say anything about a horse. Did you buy her a whole horse?”

“As opposed to a half one?” He snickered. “Yes, I sure did. She’s feisty. A real beauty—like Madeline. That’s why I hope that I didn't ruin our friendship by sleeping with her."

"A strong bond isn't that easily broken," Jonathan assured him. "If it's solid, then this is a minor hiccup. One that's repairable."

"Thanks, fellas. I'll take everything you said under advisement," he said, even as he knew he just wasn't ready to open his heart. He had his daughters to think about. They loved Madeline, and it would be traumatic if things went sour. But if they remained friends, it was a safer option. Forrest smoothed his goatee. "Speaking of repairs, I could use some assistance with the irrigation system…" Forrest then launched into the overwatering in some areas and water clogging.

"I've got you, cuz," Jonathan piped up. "I know just the person to call. Consider it handled."

His cousin was a man of his word. Forrest hung up, knowing that the problem on his property would be as good as fixed. He should have called his cousins about the irrigation system sooner, and perhaps he would have if Madeline hadn't dominated his thoughts. Somehow, he would have to find the right balance between his personal and business lives. And somehow, he had to avoid getting hurt by either one in the process.

When Madeline stepped into Francesca's Bar and Grill, the tantalizing smells reminded her that she hadn't eaten since that morning. Her sisters, Shelby and Jillian, had called an hour ago to encourage her to meet up with them for shopping and dinner. After Forrest left, she had ventured inside her condo and distracted herself by toggling between researching her father's past and reviewing details for Kate's birthday party.

That was plenty to keep her occupied until her sisters reached out. The fact that she needed groceries was her main impetus for agreeing to dinner. She didn't have the energy for shopping, although she loved spending time at ER Grocery to check out their gourmet selections. Plus, their salad bar had a vast and farm-fresh assortment. Madeline hugged Shelby and Jillian and took one of the empty seats at the table for four.

"You two are twinning today," she said, moving her curls out of her face. *Twinning.* She missed Ivy and Violet. But if she kept thinking about them, she would swim in the doldrums.

"Yes, these are fresh off the rack," Shelby said, smoothing her hands down the body of her dress. Both she and Jillian wore maxi dresses with matching slip-ons. They looked cute.

"We could have been a trio if you had come shopping with us," Jillian teased. Then she pointed at Madeline's striped shirt, white pants and sandals. "But you'll do."

"I wasn't in the best of moods and I would have been poor company," Madeline supplied, scooting her chair closer to the table.

"What's going on?" Jillian asked.

She shrugged. "Nothing I want to get into. I don't want to bring y'all down. But I *do* want to eat. Did you order already?" she asked, changing the topic on purpose. Madeline couldn't bear to see the pity on their faces when they heard about her latest relationship bust.

Her sisters took the hint. Jillian picked up her menu. "No, but we did order spinach dip with chips."

"And salsa," Shelby added.

Her stomach grumbled. "Yum!" she said with forced cheer.

Shelby snapped to attention and tilted her head to look behind Madeline. "Hang on a sec. Is that—" She waved vigorously. "Hayes and Penn just walked in."

Seconds later, her brothers joined them and then a shuffling of chairs ensued as the server added two settings. Before he left, he took their drink orders. Everyone requested water with lemon, except for Shelby and Madeline, who chose sweet tea.

"So, I've been researching since we learned about Dad being on his own from such a young age. I can't imagine how he survived without any relatives to take him in." Her grandparents' small parcel of land had been foreclosed upon their passing, so he hadn't had a place to live either. She glanced at the other four occupants at the table. "And I'm dying to know how our father went from being orphaned with no money or home to becoming a millionaire by twenty-five."

"Gosh, he was so young," Jillian remarked.

"Yes, but how he went from working to survive to a millionaire is a big mystery that I'd like to solve."

Jillian tapped her temple. "I wonder if he inherited a ranch from one of those places he worked."

"I looked into that," Madeline told her. "But Dad didn't inherit any property."

"To be honest with you," Hayes added, "I'm mystified."

"I'm pretty clueless myself," Penn said.

The server returned with their drinks and appetizer before taking their food orders and collecting the menus.

Madeline sipped some of her sweet tea, then held up her glass. "Well, let's all keep digging until we get some answers."

"Agreed," Penn said. They all clinked glasses and chattered about what was going on with their lives.

Madeline's cell phone vibrated in her pants' pocket, and she pulled it out and saw that it was Forrest calling. Her pulse quickened; she so badly wanted to answer the call but she didn't know what he wanted to say and how she would react, so it was better she wait. She sent it to voicemail and placed her phone face down on the table. She would return his call when she was back at home and away from prying eyes. The phone went off again, and this time she put it on silent and dropped it in her bag.

It took a second for her to realize that the table had gone quiet.

"Is everything good?" Shelby asked, concerned.

Madeline scanned the four sets of eyes waiting to hear what she had to say. "Yeah. It's all good." She placed a hand on her chest. "Gosh, I'm not used to having siblings."

Hayes reached across the table to squeeze her hand. "Yes, you've got brothers to protect you if needed."

"And your sisters, too," Jillian said, jabbing Hayes in the ribs.

Hayes held up his hands. "Alright. You're *all* capable women, but Penn and I are here to support you no matter what."

Madeline smiled. "Despite the circumstances, I'm so glad I have you all in my life. I really didn't know what I was missing until I met you guys and getting to know you all made all the terrible things our father did bearable."

"All the more reason to find the sixth sibling," Shelby said.

"That's true," Penn chimed in. "And we will succeed. Together."

The next evening, Madeline entered the beautiful grounds of the Emerald Ridge Hotel to meet with their event planner. The plan was that, though the amusement park would be open throughout the day, the official start time for Kate's birthday party would be 5:00 p.m. at this very hotel.

Though they had already confirmed that the date was open through email and phone conversations, Madeline hadn't yet signed the official contract. Her aim was to get that done, plus get the floorplan configurations so she could coordinate with the designer and decorators. She also just needed to see and feel the space in person.

The coordinator greeted her, and they proceeded into the grand ballroom.

"The entrance is deceiving. It looks like it can easily fit four hundred people in here." Her voice echoed in the empty space. "It can actually hold up to six hundred comfortably. We also can mount cameras and screens so that everyone has access to the lady of the hour."

Madeline tilted her head to take in the sculpted ceiling, walls, and the ornate chandelier. "That is exquisite."

"We've recently renovated and we're proud of the results," the coordinator preened.

They visited the overflow rooms, which she would use for predinner cocktails as well as the dance floor. With each step, her vision and enthusiasm for Kate's event grew. "I can set up a vintage photo booth in here." She clasped her hands. "This is going to be a party to remember." She looked at the woman beside her. "Let's get all the contract details settled, and then we can talk menus."

"Alright, we'll head to my office. Our culinary manager has already left for the day but we can schedule the menu tasting, and I can have her send you options in the meantime."

"This sounds like so much fun.I already know I am going to want to taste *everything*."

Chapter Eight

Hey. Can you talk?

Madeline had been awake since 4:00 a.m. and had spent the past hour working on the vendor applications for Kate's birthday party when her phone pinged. Her traitorous heart skipped a beat when she saw it was a text message from Forrest. Shoot, she had stayed out too late with her brothers and sisters to return his calls from the night before.

But maybe that had been a good thing. Maybe it was okay to make him sweat a bit, especially after his funk the day before. However, she was curious to know what Forrest wanted to talk to her about. Plus, she missed her friend. And that was reason enough to reach out. Instead of texting, she pressed the outgoing call button.

"Madeline. You called…" he said, sounding somewhat surprised.

"Of course, I did. Why wouldn't I?" she asked.

"It's just you didn't pick up yesterday…" He trailed off.

This was where she would fill in the blanks on her whereabouts the day before. Well, that was not going to happen. Let him wonder. Let him sweat. *Mister I Just*

Want to be Friends. “I was busy. But I don’t think you wanted to talk about that?”

“No, I, uh, I wanted to apologize,” Forrest said, sounding unsure.

Good. He deserved to feel just as off-balance as she did. Any other time, Madeline would let it go, but she had strong feelings for him, and he was treating them like a game.

“I also wanted to ask if you wanted to go for a ride with me this morning. Junie is here with the children, so it would just be the two of us.” His voice dipped. “We’ll have a chance to talk.”

Talk? Hmm…that could mean so many things. Though she was still mad at him, she thanked him for the apology and agreed to go for a ride with him. For one thing, she was already in love with that horse. For another, she had plenty she wanted to *talk* about after he had groveled a bit. “I’ll meet you at the stables in an hour.” Madeline dressed with speed.

The sun was already pouring out its fury on the earth when Madeline arrived at Forrest’s ranch. When she got out and scanned the property, her breath caught at the sheer beauty of his land. Forrest devoted a lot of time to taking care of his home, and it showed. Everything from the lush greens and melded wire fencing to sturdy barns with high, barrel-wood ceilings, the main home and caretaker quarters had been designed with luxury and durability in mind. Only the best for the Porter men.

A light breeze teased at her hair, though judging by the temperature already, today would be another scorcher, which was why she had chosen a lightweight, long-sleeved top, jeans and riding boots. She’d finished off her look with her red bandana around her neck and a new Stetson on her head.

Madeline got to the stable before he did, which allowed her the pleasure of checking him out as he approached. The checkered shirt, jeans and black riding boots draped his frame, emphasizing those strong arms, flat torso, and that daggone sexy swagger. Forrest looked like he belonged on the cover of a magazine. Her mouth went dry. Dang, she knew how every inch of him felt.

When he drew close, he tapped her Stetson with his index finger. "Thanks for meeting me." Then he raked his hands through his curls, pinned those gorgeous brown eyes on her, and gave her a crooked smile.

How could she resist?

Whitt, a tall, lean, brown-skinned man with shoulder-length locks, brought out their horses. She took in Temperance and went over to rub the horse's hind legs. "You're a beauty."

"Careful with her now—she's got spirit," Whitt said, though his attention was clearly on Forrest. Her cheeks warmed; it was obvious that Whitt wasn't talking about the horse.

"I plan to be," Forrest said, meeting her gaze. His horse sidled up next to him, and he patted Samson with affection.

Whitt looked between them and then cleared his throat. "I've got work to do," he said, rushing back into the stables, leaving them alone. Temperance trotted over, swishing her tail, a sign that the mare liked the stallion.

The two horses rubbed noses and Madeline arched her brow. "It seems we are witnessing a match in the making," she said, letting out a little laugh.

He chuckled and dropped his voice. “Is that what it is?”

“Yup, and I’m here for it.”

Forrest moved closer to her and lightly grabbed her shirt. She pulled away. They had to clear the air before they could cozy up like the horses. Putting distance between them, Forrest got on his horse, then gestured to her to do the same. Forrest kicked his heels and his horse broke into a trot.

After a brief hesitation, she mounted Temperance. The mare protested, so she tugged on the reins. Temperance kicked her hind legs, but Madeline tightened her grip and hugged the horse, stroking her mane. Several minutes passed before Temperance settled.

“Okay, girl. It’s time to ride.” She joined Forrest, who hovered by the fence.

“Ha! Well, you can watch the rear of my back instead.” He took off, dust spewing in his wake.

“Oh, he thinks because he was some fancy rodeo star that he can outrun me.” She hunkered down and prodded Temperance into a gallop. Seconds later, she scooched past Forrest, satisfied at his mouth dropping open. She giggled. “Catch me if you can!”

Forrest dipped low in the saddle, a determined look on his face. Together, Samson and Temperance ran free as they crossed the expanse of his property.

Later, while the horses rested by the creek, Forrest and Madeline finally addressed his behavior.

“I acted unseemly,” he said, sifting a finger through the grass. “I shouldn’t have been so cold toward you when you didn’t do anything to me.”

Her chest eased and she rested her head on his shoulder. “I accept your apology.”

He shifted to look at her, placing a hand on each of her shoulders. "You forgive me? Just like that?"

She touched his cheek. "Yes. Just like that. We're friends, right? That means I can give you some grace." She sighed. "This is a lot to process. I don't think either of us really saw 'us' coming, but I'm happy it did."

"You're right…and I'm, uh, just kind of at a loss for how to navigate what happened in Houston." His eyes looked troubled.

"You mean when we made love?" she challenged. Because that was what it had been for her. And for him, too, she hoped.

"Yes… Then." He paused for a beat. "But now I'm worried that things will feel too tense. Too *different*. Maybe we need to take a step back and reevaluate."

Her stomach dropped and she leaned away from him. "Forrest, what are you saying? You said you didn't regret sleeping with me, so I'm confused." *And hurt. Like nobody's business.*

"I don't regret one of the most earthshattering nights of my life. But I'm saying we complicated things when we had sex—so maybe's it's not a good idea for us to go there again. Let's just make it a one and done, and move on."

Wow. She had to remind herself that Forrest had no idea what that night had meant to her. "Our night together didn't complicate things for *me*. It did quite the opposite. It made me realize how good we are together."

"My heart is closed right now. I have to focus on my daughters."

Pain splintered her heart. Just when she opened herself up to another man, he didn't want to do the same. Love was not her fortune. "I'll respect your wishes," she whispered. "But please don't let fear dictate your actions."

His brows furrowed and his eyes troubled. "Friendship is all I have the bandwidth to give."

How could he sound so final about an experience that had been so unforgettable? That twisted her gut to know he didn't think she was worth fighting for. But she was his friend first and would try to adhere to his boundaries even if she disagreed. Next of all, Madeline wasn't about to plead with a man to stay with her as if she were desperate. She inhaled and squared her shoulders. "Alright. Friends, it is," she said before releasing a long, despondent sigh.

His equally long sigh was the only thing that pacified her a bit.

And Madeline held to that bargain for an entire week, even when she saw they were both miserable. All she could hope was that things would eventually return to normal. They hung out at each other's houses, avoiding physical contact unless absolutely necessary, which made things tense and awkward between them. And she had to catch herself to keep from staring at him and then pretend she didn't notice him staring at her.

It was just one hot mess.

But Forrest was too stubborn to admit it wasn't working; and they couldn't go backward. She couldn't *un*fall out of love with him. She couldn't forget the tenderness of his touch. Her only respite was that she hadn't declared how she felt, even though that truth was coming to a boil and it would be a matter of time before it spilled over.

He stood by the window of his living room and peered outside. The girls were still down for their naps but would be getting up soon. Man, he couldn't recall the last time it had rained so hard and for such a long time. But the weather was the perfect backdrop for Forrest's current state of mind. He and Madeline had made plans to take the girls to the special playground and wanted to review the finishing touches on the replica of Cowboy Country USA before their mother picked them up. But the torrent had changed those plans, so they were meeting up for a movie and popcorn instead.

Tension rode his back and shoulders, which made him irritable and snappy with his workers. In short, he was miserable.

However, Forrest was determined to keep up a brave front. Besides, the ache in his chest was a consequence of his own decision. *His* fear of repeating the past. He couldn't cave after a mere seven days even if desire charged through his body whenever Madeline was in his vicinity. It didn't help that his nights had been filled with flashbacks of their time together. He tortured himself remembering all the things they had done to each other and how their bodies had fit so well together…like spoons.

A cry on his baby monitor snapped him out of his thoughts. Forrest dragged a hand through his hair and trudged upstairs to his daughters' room. Junie was already there, changing Violet's diaper. Ivy was still asleep with her bum in the air. His heart melted at the sight of them. *His daughters. His family.* They had to be his main priority. Not his libido. Ivy stretched and popped one eye open. She gave him a toothy, drooly smile.

"Hey, sweetheart," he said, playing with her feet. "Did you have a good nap?" He reached for a diaper and wipes. Junie went to dispose of the diaper. Violet used that opportunity to start jumping on her bed. "Settle down, Violet. I don't want you to fall."

Giggling, she continued jumping again until Junie scooped her up. "Did you want me to feed them before Madeline comes by?"

"No, we're planning on making homemade pizzas with the girls." He cocked his head. "You can take the rest of the afternoon off if you need."

"I'll take you up on that. My mother hasn't been doing well, and I need to go check on her since my brother is sick." Junie's mother had been diagnosed with early dementia.

"I'm sorry to hear that. Let me know if I can do anything for you."

Just then Cora called, asking if she could come get the girls early due to the bad weather. Forrest told her that was fine. She said she would be there within the hour. He would have to let Madeline know that there would be a change in plans. There was a crack of thunder before another downpour. Yes, Madeline should definitely stay in, instead of venturing out in this weather. He fired off a text.

Hey, it's bad out there. Raincheck?

But then Junie captured his attention.

"I'll get the girls packed up so I can leave before Cora gets here." Forrest noticed that she appeared to be on the verge of tears. Junie then shared how scared she was to lose her mother, her only living parent. As he offered words of comfort, Forrest thought of Madeline, who had lost her father. She had cried inconsolably on his shoulders when she'd heard the news. He hadn't known the right words to say, but he had rocked her to sleep on his couch.

Death was inevitable, but he didn't relish how it showed up uninvited. Forrest was grateful his parents were still alive and healthy—something not to take for granted. He made a mental note to check in on them more often. Between his daughters and the business, most of his time was already spoken for. But as Madeline had pointed out, Forrest needed to be intentional about carving out the time. And, really, there was no time like the present.

He took out his cell phone to call his mother, as his father was most likely watching the playoffs. As he waited for her to answer, he strolled into his kitchen to double-check the ingredients that he'd had delivered earlier that morning. There was pizza flour, sauce and three kinds of cheese, along with a variety of toppings. This was their second attempt. The first had been disastrous with soggy dough, but it had been fun. Hopefully, tonight would be better, but he did have the local pizzeria flyer on standby.

"Hey, son. It's good hearing from you," Rosie said. He could hear the sound of water running and figured she was in the kitchen washing dishes as usual. Or rather, *rewashing* dishes. That chore was her favorite pastime.

"I was just calling to check up on you," he said, hating how forlorn he sounded. But if he knew his mother, she would pick up on his tone and urge him to start talking. Sure enough, the sounds of water stopped.

"We're good over here. Your father is yelling at the TV and sneak-eating some fried chicken wings that he bought from the supermarket." Rosie had his father on a rigid diet regimen after Duke'd had a "heart event" the summer before. His father had called him a few times to protest, but Forrest was on his mother's side. Duke needed to give up his love for fried food and sodas. "What's wrong?" she asked, then fired off another question. "Is it Ivy and Violet? Are they okay?"

"Mom, everyone is *fine*. I literally just called to see how you are doing."

The water went on again. A signal that all was right in her world. "Oh, okay. For a second there, you sounded like a lost puppy, and you flared up my anxiety levels like you did when you were a kid. I swear, I couldn't turn my back on you for a minute. You were always getting into something. Speaking of always getting into something, how are my grandbabies doing? The last time they were here, they kept me on my toes."

That made him laugh. Forrest recounted the lotion escapade with his girls. His mother snorted. "At least they didn't douse themselves with ink, the way you did. I don't know what possessed Duke to buy a pen with ink pot with a toddler in the house. Said he was trying to do calligraphy. That man and his hobbies are driving me up the wall. The latest is some kind of weaving, so once again, he is redesigning the shed."

His father was always trying something new, and when he did, Duke went all out. He was usually really good at it, but then he would lose interest.

The water was still running. There couldn't be that many dirty dishes. "Mom, what are you washing so long? There are only two of you in the house."

"Oh, I am cleaning the silverware." Another task she did when she was worried.

"What's going on?" he asked gently.

"Nothing. Your father has his checkup with his cardiologist, and that has me on edge."

Ah, that explained it. "Dad will be alright, Mom. What time is it? I'll meet you at the doctor's tomorrow."

"Oh, you're such a good son. I'll text you the details, and kiss Ivy and Violet for me."

At the peal of the doorbell, he ended the call with, "Tell Dad I said hello and I'll see him tomorrow." He was on his way to the front door when, from his peripheral vision, he could see Junie coming down with the girls. She had one in her arms, and the other she was guiding down the stairs. He rushed over to help her and then answered the door. Junie retreated, stating she would leave through the back door. Dang, she really wanted to avoid Cora.

His ex-wife followed him inside the foyer. "Mommyyyy!" the girls squealed, wrapping their arms around her legs.

Forrest leaned against the banister. "It's coming down out there. You probably should have waited until tomorrow morning."

"Yes, but I missed the girls and…" She squinted and gave him the once-over. "You look like you could use a break. Frankly, you look miserable."

"Speak for yourself," he snapped. "How I look or feel is none of your business. You need only concern yourself with the twins." His words were harsh, and he regretted them the minute they left his mouth.

Cora held up her hands. "Excuse me for caring. I'll get out of your hair." She brushed past him and snatched up the baby bag.

"Cora, I'm so sorry. I don't even know why I went off on you like that."

"Keep your apology. It's all good."

He went over to help with the girls, but she rebuffed him. He shoved his hands in his pockets and quietly kissed his girls. "I'll see you next time."

Ivy touched his face. "Daddy sad." All he could do was nod and hug his daughters. He felt like an ogre.

"Mmm-hmm," Cora said, her voice brittle. "I guess it's okay when they say it." Holding their hands, she sailed through the door. He could hear his girls calling for him since he would normally accompany them to help buckle them into their mom's Mercedes. But the hurt on Cora's face held him back. The rain had tapered off a bit, so at least they wouldn't get drenched without his assistance.

He stood waving at the door until her car disappeared around the bend. Then, with a heavy heart, he went back inside.

The doorbell rang again. Scurrying, he yanked the door open, thinking Cora had forgotten something. If so, he would use that opportunity to apologize once more for his obscene behavior. Madeline stood there, looking adorable in her blue poncho.

Tension drained from his body just at the sight of her.

He shooed her inside, eyeing the puddle at her feet. "You still came…"

"I didn't see your text until I was in your driveway, so…" Madeline's hair, stuffed under a cap, drooped like wet noodles. She had on a blue cami and jean shorts with a pair of sneakers, and to Forrest, she had never looked cuter.

"You just missed the girls." He averted his eyes because that cami was soaked, providing a tantalizing display. She wasn't wearing a bra. Darn it, the woman didn't fight fair.

She wrung her hands and then crossed them over her breasts. "Do you want me to leave?"

"No," he shot out. "No. We can still hang out and catch a movie. Friends do that all the time."

"Um, sure." She lifted her shoulders, her breasts swaying with the motion…and his mouth went dry. "I'm not sure how to navigate backtracking to friendship. Especially since I honestly don't want to." He took in her lush lashes and those moist, glossy lips, and prayed for strength. He would put some distance between them on the couch.

"We'll figure it out." He curled his fingers into a loose fist to keep from snatching her close to him.

They decided to order pizza, made popcorn and then selected a Sandra Bullock romcom since it was her turn to choose. He put on the surround sound and sat at the furthest end of the couch, putting as much space as possible between them.

Madeline wasn't going for that. She slid down next to him, cuddling into his chest, and Lord knew, it felt… right. She was where she was meant to be. That twisted his gut. He placed a hand on her thigh, and she burrowed deeper into him. She felt so soft, and her hair smelled like peaches. Memories of their night together came rushing back, and he stuffed his hand into the popcorn to keep from reaching for her. Somehow, he kept his hands off her throughout the movie, but every time she slipped popcorn between those lips, he had to stifle a groan.

And now that they were chowing down on pizza, it wasn't much better. It was *worse*. Watching her flick that cheese on her tongue almost undid him. He was sure she could see the sweat beads forming across his forehead.

She toyed with the buttons on his shirt. "So, since you're on your own for a few days, how about we hang out together tomorrow? I'm touring Leonetti Vineyards with that marketing maven, Gia Leonetti. I'm thinking about using their vineyard as an event venue for my business. It might be fun trying out the different wines."

"Uh… I can't." He cleared his throat. "I'm supposed to accompany my mother to my father's doctor's appointment."

She turned her head to face him. "Is everything alright?"

"It's just a checkup with his cardiologist. At least, I hope that's all it is." Anxiety flooded his body, and he released a long breath.

"Call or text me if you need," Madeline offered.

The concern in those beautiful green depths made him second-guess his decision to just be friends. Because right now, he wanted to press his lips to hers and relive their night together. Her eyes darkened. She must have read his mind. Maybe they could have one more night. That wouldn't cause irreparable harm, right? Then they could go back to the way things were before. He reached out to play with her hair, but she rested a hand on his chest and shook her head.

"Listen, I can't do the whole 'friends with benefits' thing. I'm not cut out for that. We're either *together* together or we're not." Her brow rose. "So which one is it?"

Forrest shrank away from her and helped himself to another slice of pizza to give himself thinking time.

"Hello?"

"I respect your position, but I'm a proven failure at relationships, and if I have to choose, I'd rather not jeopardize our friendship."

"I see." She avoided his gaze. "I've got a long day tomorrow. I'd best be heading home." She took her time gathering her belongings on purpose. Waiting for him to recant, to stop her from leaving. But the sound was the squish of her still very wet sneakers as she walked out the door the same way she had entered. Alone.

Chapter Nine

At eight the next morning, Madeline entered her storefront located on Central Avenue, holding a box of baked goods from the Emerald Ridge Bakery. She turned on the lights, scanned the space, and puffed her chest. The renovations had finally been completed, and she was pleased with the final product. She had overseen every painstaking detail to create a posh, fun space.

Today was her first official day conducting business here instead of at her home office space, which she was going to convert back into a guest room. Madeline was moving on four hours of sleep, but she had a meeting with a potential VIP client that Kate had recommended before going to the Leonetti Vineyard and had to bring her A game. So, she was going to need at least two cups of coffee. Madeline marched over to her coffee and pastry area and placed the baked goods on the counter. Once she started up the Keurig and heard the satisfying hiss of the grounds brewing, she scanned her space.

The walls were beige with mint-green trimmings, and the reception area had a mix of chairs and plush couches with plants in each corner of the room. On the walls were a couple of abstract watercolor art pieces, along with huge framed displays highlighting events she had done in the past. There was a welcome desk—which she hoped would be filled with an assistant one day—but for now, she and Holly had offices in the back of the store.

Madeline took a few pictures of the exterior and interior, sent them to her mom and then posted them to her social pages, making sure to tag Holly. She bit her bottom lip. Should she tag Forrest, too?

Of course, she should. They were still *best buds*. Ugh.

After she had thrown that proposition at Forrest the night before, though she'd known he would turn her down, she had been disappointed that he hadn't rooted for them. She had spent the night replaying a lot of their encounters, wondering how she'd ended up falling for a man who seemed determined to keep her in a tiny emotional box.

Their connection, the way they clicked like matching puzzle pieces, wasn't something that happened often. Even their horses were in sync, so she had hoped that Forrest would grab onto it, but he'd been burned by love too many times to take a risk. Hurt, Madeline had made her excuses and gone home.

The question she kept asking herself was why she kept torturing herself like this. But she already knew the answer. They were friends, and she had promised herself that nothing would interfere with that. Not even her wayward heart.

There was a FaceTime from Taffy. Her mother's face was covered in a thick, gooey substance.

"I'm surprised you're calling me in the midst of your spa day," Madeline said. Her mother did those often and Madeline had enjoyed those mother-daughter sessions.

"I had to," Taffy said. "Your *little* storefront looks positively darling."

She frowned. Only her mother would give a compliment thinly laced with an insult.

"It's what I could afford, Mother."

"Whenever you use Mother and that tone, I know you're tiffed at me. But since you insist on playing the struggling startup role, then that's on you."

"I wanted to do it on my own. Why can't you be just be proud of me?" she ground out.

"I am." She flailed her hands. "I'm just saying you could have opened up on a much grander scale. And you are very much a Fortune."

"I want to succeed without obvious nepotism."

"You can't change who you are, so you might as well ride that nepo train and give the princess wave." Her mother demonstrated the wave with a wide smile.

Madeline wanted to point out that she looked more like a smashed avocado than royalty, but why get catty when Taffy meant well. But then Taffay added, "Now, quit scowling or you'll get wrinkles."

"That's not how it works, Mom. There's no avoiding them as we age."

"As if? I plan to get snatched like Momma Kardashian if that time comes." Hearing her name, Taffy blew air kisses. "Toodles. I've got to go, but congrats, honey."

Rubbing her temples, Madeline sighed, feeling a little deflated at Taffy's slight condescension. But then her phone dinged with text messages and emojis from Holly.

OMG!! I love it!! I love our new space. I can't believe you didn't tell me. We are back, baby!!

Madleline cracked up and sent a response.

I couldn't tell you or it wouldn't be a surprise!! XOXO. Talk soon.

A few seconds later, Forrest's name popped up on her screen. Her stomach clenched.

I'm so proud of you. You did it!! We must celebrate later.

Her smile slipped, because she was sure his idea of a celebration was quite different from hers, but she gave the messages a thumbs-up. Then she followed her nose to get her first cup of coffee and get started on her day.

The meeting with her prospective client for an engagement party ended with a signed contract and a large down payment.

Hope flooded her chest as she drove to the Leonetti Vineyards to meet with Gia. It was only ten minutes from the center of Emerald Ridge. The vineyard was a century-old family winery run by the Leonetti family. This was *real*. She was making her comeback, one event at a time. If all went well, she might end up securing this venue for the engagement party. Gosh, she loved it when things came together like this. Now, if only she could master that in her love life.

Madeline turned into the property, which was a half-mile-long road. She admired the lush, manicured greenery and the view was simply breathtaking.

Gia Leonetti stood waiting when she pulled up. The tall, slender brunette was dressed in an elegant cream pantsuit and black pumps. Madeline and Gia exchanged air kisses and then, arm in arm, began the tour. The winery resembled a gorgeous Tuscan villa with the family mansion tucked between the winery buildings.

They rounded the corner and spotted four people walking toward them. “Oh, there’s Bella.” She squeezed Madeline’s hand before waving the group over.

“Bella’s my vintner sister, and those are my grandparents, and I don’t know who that fourth person is, but we’ll find out soon enough,” Gia explained. Once they were close, she introduced Madeline to Bella, as well as to the Leonetti matriarch and grandfather. Then Bella presented her to the fourth person, Oliver Webb. Oliver was a rancher from Austin, Texas. He was tall and muscular, with dark hair and dressed in typical rancher garb with a white Stetson. A round of handshakes occurred.

“My mother, Lesley Webb, used to live in Emerald Ridge long ago,” Oliver offered, his brown eyes warm and friendly. “I’m hoping to meet people who knew her.”

Madeline nodded. “It’s a pleasure to meet you. I’m sorry, but I’ve never heard of her.”

“I haven’t heard of a Lesley Webb either,” Gia added.

“That’s okay. That’s why I’m in town playing amateur sleuth,” Oliver said with a laugh. “She loved wines and had a large collection, so I figure that my mother must have visited Leonetti Vineyards before I was born and moved away.”

Seeing the blank looks on Gia’s grandparents’ faces made Madeline secretly believe that Oliver’s search would be futile, because the Leonettis had lived in Emerald Ridge for quite some time, and if they didn’t know Lesley… But she didn’t want to discourage the man, so she said, “I wish you all the success in your quest.”

Once they were out of earshot, Gia blew a raspberry.

"Something tells me that Oliver would have much more luck trying to grow a pinot noir grape than finding his mother." If Gia hadn't already explained how difficult pinot noir grapes were to cultivate during the tour, Madeline wouldn't have gotten that analogy. Apparently, that type of grape had sensitivity to certain soils, pruning and winemaking techniques as well as climate conditions.

Thinking of her own quest to dig up information about her father and their sixth sibling, Madeline's heart went out to Oliver. She just hoped he would have made better progress than she had so far.

Even though Duke had assured him that the cardiac examination was a routine procedure, that didn't stop Forrest from worrying about his father. He sat with his mother in the outpatient area, waiting for the cardiologist to provide an update, and praying for good news.

Duke had had arrhythmia for years, which hadn't been a cause of concern, but recently his father had complained of heart palpitations and minor chest pain, so his doctor wanted to monitor him more closely.

"He should almost be finished," Rosie said, her lips quivering. "Hopefully, this will all be for nothing." On the way to the appointment, she had been upbeat and appeared unbothered by the visit, but he was now realizing that show had all been for his father's benefit. And Duke had pretty much done the same thing, cracking jokes the entire ride over. The love his parents had for each other was unparalleled.

"I'm sure we're worrying for nothing. Dad probably just needs to lay off the pizzas and chicken wings." He slipped an arm around his mother's shoulders. It wasn't often that Forrest saw his mother scared.

Rosie shook her head. "He claims he's running an errand, so he can get his fix. I keep telling him it's not good for his heart." She nervously twisted her necklace. "We've been together for over thirty years, and it's not enough."

Wow. To Forrest, thirty years felt like a lifetime, and to hear his mother utter those words profoundly impacted him. He would love to feel that way about someone. Like…with Madeline? Could she be his forever person if he opened his heart? However, there was a flip side, because the anxiety his mother was experiencing was very real.

"Dad will be around for longer than that, Mom. I'm sure of it." The minute the words left his mouth, Forrest berated himself. He couldn't promise that when he wasn't sure what the outcome of Duke's appointment was. Yet his words brought Rosie the comfort she needed.

Her lips lifted into a smirk. "Yeah, I agree. He's surprising me with an anniversary trip to Italy, so I know he's not about to miss out on that."

Forrest laughed. "Yes, Dad is way too stubborn." He didn't bother to ask how his mother knew about the surprise. Nothing got past Rosie Porter. That's why she was perfect for his father.

Rosie jabbed his ribs with her index finger. "And you're just like him. When you make up your mind about something, it's hard for you to let it go."

He cocked his head. "Some would call that a desirable trait."

"It is." She scoffed. "Except for when you're dead wrong."

Now Forrest hadn't mentioned anything about his and Madeline's relationship—or lack of—so he had no clue what his mother was referring to. He hadn't said a word to his father, either, so there was no way that information had funneled back to her. "What are you talking about?" he hedged.

"You and Madeline," she shot back, giving him a pat on his arm. "You're too mule-headed to see that she should be more than a friend, but your father told me to mind my business, so I'm not saying a word."

Except she had.

Forrest was spared a response when the cardiologist beckoned to them. "He's right in here."

"What's going on?" his mother asked.

"He wants to tell you himself." He ushered them to the door before wishing Duke well. "I'll see you in three months."

They followed him into the room. His father was stretched out on the bed with a huge look of relief on his face. "I'm alright. I just need to lay off the caffeine and salty foods, and continue my exercise regimen." Duke had an in-house gym that he used twice a day. His father had instilled a love of fitness in him from when he was a child. Clapping her hands, Rosie peppered Duke's face with kisses.

Forrest grinned as relief seeped through him. "I'm going to send you over a private chef."

His father only nodded, distracted by his wife, who now held his face in her hands. "Now, if you'll excuse me, son. I'd love to give my wife a kiss not fit for your eyes."

"Happy to give you some privacy," Forrest joked, shielding his eyes. He ducked out of the room, telling his parents that he would wait in the truck, but they were too caught up in each other to hear him. As happy as he was that his parents still loved each other after all those years, a twinge of longing pierced his heart. He wanted what they had. And Forrest could actually have that kind of never-ending spark with Madeline if the fear of a second relationship failing hadn't held him back.

His cell buzzed with a text message from Madeline.

How did everything go with your dad?

A smile touched his lips. She was so thoughtful and kind. He hurried to respond.

He's okay. Just needs to watch what he eats.

Good. I'm relieved to hear that.

Going to get him a personal chef.

Excellent idea. So, no more Porter cuts for him?

He snickered.

Yeah, that won't go over too well. Everything in moderation. See you later?

Definitely.

Cora called, cutting into his convo with Madeline. He answered cautiously, remembering how mad she'd been with him when she'd left. "Hey, I need to ask you a favor."

He started up the truck and put on the AC, because

the sun was in full force, then settled back into his seat. "What's up?"

"So, Dean surprised me with a getaway. A deluxe train ride across the country, and I've always wanted to do that." She cleared her throat. "I wondered if I could drop off the girls early?"

Now it was on the tip of his tongue to remind Cora of how she had reacted when he'd asked her to change the schedule so he could attend Madeline's high school reunion, but he resisted the temptation. That would be petty—and he would never say no to anything concerning his daughters if he could.

"I don't want to inconvenience you…" She trailed off.

"Ivy and Violet are never an inconvenience. I'm out and about, but you can bring them by later."

She released a long breath. "Okay, thanks so much. I'll get their bags packed."

"No need. I have everything they need."

When they ended the call, Forrest made sure to reach out to Madeline.

Hey! Change of plans. I'm going to have the girls. Raincheck?

The dots on his phone signaled that she was typing something. But when the response came in, it was simply,

OK, cool, best bud.

Forrest figured she must have deleted what she'd really wanted to say. He found himself disappointed at her blasé response. It felt like how a regular friend would respond, and her use of the words *best bud* made him grit his teeth. But that was what he'd insisted he wanted, so he had no right to feel any way.

His parents came out of the entrance. Forrest put the vehicle in gear and went to the roundabout to help get them settled. His father sat in front with him and his mother in the rear seat, saying she could keep an eye on Duke from there.

On the way to their home, Forrest promised to bring the girls by for a visit. Both were keen to see Ivy and Violet. His father was already talking about grilling the usual suspects, even conceding when Rosie added salmon and salad to the mix. His mother's tone suggested there was no talking his way into eating something else.

Duke opened his mouth, and Forrest knew he was about to protest. He patted his father's back. "Too soon, Dad. Too soon." Duke clenched his jaw but didn't say a word. If he knew his father, that wouldn't last long. He could hear him muttering under his breath the entire ride and even when Forrest walked them inside their home, he was still fussing to himself.

Rosie rolled her eyes. "He'll be alright once he puts on the sports channel." Then she proceeded to pack Forrest a to-go container of steak, baked potato and green beans, saying, "Your father won't need this tonight, but don't let him see you taking it outside."

"Got it." He gave her a thumbs-up then yelled out to his father that he was leaving.

"Let's go riding soon," Duke called out.

His mother mouthed, *No way.*

"Alright. We'll see about that," Forrest responded, avoiding Rosie's glare.

Whistling, Forrest left his parents' home with his food tucked under his arm, feeling optimistic. He was grateful that his father's heart condition wasn't acute. His optimism was further fueled by his cousin texting to confirm that the irrigation issue on his plot of land had been resolved.

All was right in his world. His good mood boosted his adrenaline, and Forrest eyed the clock in his truck. He had just enough time to take Samson out for a ride before Cora came with the girls.

However, when he entered the stable, memories of his last visit with Madeline assailed his mind. Temperance seemed to be looking for her, and Samson was acting like he didn't want to go anywhere without the mare. Daggone it! Madeline had ruined his all-time favorite pastime. He released a breath. Okay, he couldn't blame her for his finicky animals or for transposing his feelings onto them.

One thing he had prided himself on was always being honest with himself. And the truth was, it wasn't the horses. It was *him.* He didn't want to go riding without her, which saddened him. It was obvious he hadn't learned his lesson with Cora.

Forrest contented himself with brushing down both horses and feeding them treats before strolling back to the main house. It was a beautiful evening, with the temperature now in the low seventies, and a light breeze that was most welcome.

Cora was already in his driveway, unbuckling their daughters from their car seats. He rushed to assist. They entered his home, each carrying one of the girls.

"I'll call them later to wish them good-night," Cora said, moving toward the front door.

Forrest put on the television and called out to her,. "Wait, hang on a second." He jogged over to where she stood. "I wanted to apologize for my attitude yesterday. I shouldn't have snapped at you like that."

She wrapped a hand around his arm. "I accept your apology." Her large engagement ring sparkled under the lights. There was a time when the sight of that would cause resentment to surface. But now, he didn't care at all. *Progress.*

"There's something else I need to tell you." He squared his shoulders. It was time to get this off his chest so he could face her without guilt.

"I went somewhere with Madeline and there were some women who assumed she was the twins' mother, but I did nothing to correct them."

Cora waved a hand. "That's nothing. Our girls call Dean 'Papa' all the time."

Jealousy twisted his gut before he rebuked that sentiment. Dean was good to his daughters, and he loved them. They were fortunate to have a bonus dad, and it was time he accepted that.

"Ah, I thought about what you said about my butting into your private life, and I realized that you were right." She held out a hand. "Maybe it's time we called a truce."

They shook hands. But then she said something that gave him a jolt. "But if I may add my one cent, I was wrong about not keeping Madeline out of your life. I'm happy for you. Truly happy that you have opened your heart again."

Forrest jumped. *Had he done that?* That was odd, considering he was doing all he could to keep his heart closed. Cora continued the conversation, unaware that her last comment had rattled him. "Do you have plans for the girls' second birthday as yet?"

He shook his head. "I haven't. Did you want to do something together or give them separate birthdays again?" With all the upheaval in their relationship, Forrest had thrown a barbecue for his daughters' first birthday, refusing to celebrate with Cora and Dean. But time had a way of working everything out.

"I'd love us to do their birthdays together. I think it will be great for the girls to see the adults in their lives united. Maybe we can have it at that amusement park that Madeline's building." She peered up at him through her lashes. "We would invite Madeline, of course. I would like to have a conversation with her this time. A do-over. If you can get along with Dean, I can get along with the woman you love."

Love? He had to bite the inside of his cheek to keep from gasping aloud. Cora was drawing all kinds of conclusions, and he was curious to ask why. But to do so would be to invite her into his business, and he wasn't having that.

Still, Cora had left him with a lot to think about. And think about that, he did. He tossed and turned most of the night, dying to talk to Madeline about it but knowing for sure that was the one thing he couldn't do.

If she knew he was struggling with his decision, that might give her hope. A hope that he would change his mind. When he wouldn't. *Couldn't.* Because how could he ask her to trust in him when he didn't trust himself? He didn't trust that he had what it took to make her happy for a lifetime, and she sure as heck wouldn't settle for *happy for now.*

So where did that leave him?

Lonely, miserable, with a lot of cold showers in his future. And, selfishly, he hoped she was feeling the same, which was a terrible wish to have for his friend. But if she wasn't lonely, then that meant she had moved on, and that was something his heart would never be ready to hear.

Chapter Ten

There was magic in getting a good night's sleep. Madeline awakened to the sounds of birds chirping outside her window, with a smile on her lips and the sun shining on her face. She had slept as well as the twins after a full day at the playground.

Stretching, she arched her back and padded into the bathroom. According to the weather app, today was going to be a picture-perfect spring day, and Madeline intended to take full advantage of that.

She was going to start her morning by going by Forrest's land to check on the progress of the amusement park. The gala was only two months away and she wanted everything to be perfect. Then Madeline planned to make calls to the food vendors she had accepted to participate in the gala. A quick review of her spreadsheet the night before showed that she was operating well below her projected budget. That meant she could splurge even more on decorations and flowers.

It wasn't every day someone turned 100 years old, and she wanted the celebration to be momentous, like nothing Kate had ever seen before. Although, if Madeline were to ask her, she would probably say that all she wanted was to be reunited with Susannah.

Madeline had yet to hear back from the young woman. And she so hated that it would most likely arrive via snail mail. Waiting was excruciating and a lesson in patience. Opening her front door, she traipsed to the common mailbox area. She unlocked the small box, and peered inside, hoping there would be a letter from Susannah.

Empty.

She groaned. "Come on, already. Answer me!" She placed her key in her pocket and started back toward her condo.

A fancy black car approached, capturing her attention. Madeline paused to see who was moving in the neighborhood. The driver came to a sleek stop where she stood, popped the trunk, and got out to open the rear passenger door. Her forehead creased.

The door opened, and a long leg appeared. A woman got out, wearing oversized shades and a large hat shielding her face. She was dressed in a knee-length dress and flats. Madeline squealed. "Holly! You're back."

"I came straight here from the airport." Her bestie held out her arms, and Madeline rushed into her embrace, holding on tight. The driver extracted Holly's luggage from the trunk and sped off.

Tears rolled down her face as they rocked back and forth. "Gosh, I didn't know how much I missed you until just now."

"Same."

Finally, they pulled apart. "Why didn't you tell me you were coming? I would have met you at the airport and given you a ride to your place."

Holly flicked her hair. "And ruin the surprise? You know how I *love* a good surprise." She grabbed one bag and Madeline grabbed the other. "Let's get inside under the AC for a minute. Today feels like it's going to be a scorcher."

"I'm not complaining. We had a lot of rain, so I'm happy for the sunshine." They hauled the bags into the living room. "How was the flight?"

"Blessedly uneventful. I got some good sleep in first-class on that red-eye." She dipped her head toward Madeline. "What's on your agenda today?"

"I'm going by the amusement park and finalizing the food vendors." Madeline cocked her head. "Come with?"

"Sure. But let's get something to eat first." She patted her tummy. "I miss our American-sized portions."

"Sounds good."

"I'll freshen up. Be ready in a jiffy."

Madeline chuckled and suggested they go to the nearby diner. Just then Forrest texted.

Want to celebrate with the girls? I could bring them by your shop later? My parents are grilling, if you want to come?

Normally, she would be jumping to go, and trying to shift plans over with Holly. But, shoot, Forrest had made the boundary clear. A girlfriend might change plans but a *friend* would simply reschedule.

She bit her lower lip and texted him back.

Raincheck? Have work stuff with Holly.

OK. Maybe next time.

She almost caved at the sad-faced emoji, but this was good for the both of them.

Thirty minutes later, she and Holly shared a stack of plate-sized pancakes. A good number of the breakfast crowd had thinned, so there weren't many patrons inside.

"So, how have things been with Forrest since we last spoke?" Holly asked, cutting into her pancake. Syrup oozed from the sides in a nice, gooey mess. It looked so good, Madeline slapped one on her plate.

"Our friendship is fine…but things are at a standstill as far as a relationship. Forrest is too scared to take our friendship to the next level." She blew out a long breath. "I'm crushed, but I refuse to let it crush me. I'm relieved that I didn't pour my heart out to him, so at least I've been spared that humiliation."

Holly reached over to give her hand a squeeze. "Oh, honey. I'm sorry that he's being such a wimp."

"A *wimp*? After his marriage didn't work out, Forrest is understandably afraid to take another chance."

"You're defending him?" Holly waved her fork in circles. "I didn't expect that."

"Well, I'm trying to see Forrest's point of view, and I am attempting to accept how he feels. He's resolved to keep me at arm's length, and after last night, where he spurned my advances—okay, so maybe *spurned* is too strong a word, but I don't want to use the word rejected either. Ugh, I'm rambling and it's complicated. But in a nutshell, I am giving Forrest what he asked for. Take today for example. He wanted me to hang out with him and the kids, but I told him I was busy with work stuff."

"You know I would have understood. I'm rooting for you guys. Talk about cutting off your nose to spite your face," Holly pointed out. "Friend, you're giving up. You need to keep fighting for love." Then she pumped her fists. "I'm going to be on love's side every time."

"Yeah, but it's not a fight, if you're fighting alone."

"Dang. I can't argue with that." Holly lifted her shoulders. "Okay, if you're determined to let love go, then I'll respect that, even if I think you're making a mistake."

"I'm not going to be *that* girl. Desperate. Clingy." Madeline narrowed her eyes. "And I can't believe you're actually in favor of me running after a man who doesn't want to be caught."

"I've seen you with each other. You two belong together."

Madeline tapped her index finger on the table. "Forrest prefers to be in the friend zone. It's where he's most comfortable."

"Alright…alright. I surrender. I'll leave it alone." She held up her hands. "It's just I would love to see love work out for *someone…*"

Something in her tone made Madeline narrow her eyes. Her friend sounded like she was hurting. Like she had experienced heartache. "Is everything alright with you? Did something happen in Italy?"

Holly didn't quite meet her eyes. "Not something—*someone*. And, I'm not ready to talk about it. I'm not brave enough…" Her voice hitched before she squared her shoulders and cleared her throat. "But I promise when I'm ready, you'll be the first person I talk to. For now, I'll stuff my face with these really delicious pancakes." She dabbed at her eyes, shoveled a big bite into her mouth, and chewed with determination.

The thing about being miserable was that you could

spot it in someone else. Despite her bestie's fancy gear and well-made-up face, there was pain in her eyes and behind that smile.

"I get it. Take all the time you need. I'll be here for you when you need to talk." Madeline gave a small smile. "Let's change the topic to something over which we have influence."

"Yes. Let's talk about Kate's birthday party." Holly rubbed her hands together. "I'm eager to see which vendors made the cut." They spent the next twenty minutes reviewing the list and finishing off their meal.

Just as they wrapped up, that's when Forrest, his parents and his children came in.

Their server placed them in the furthest corner of the restaurant, but Madeline was in his direct line of sight—and he was soaking it all in. That glorious red hair, catching the light. Her wide smile. The deep, throaty laugh that teased his senses. When her delicate hand touched her throat, he bit back a groan. He should have sat somewhere else…but then someone else would have this delectable view.

"So, what was that about?" Duke asked as soon as the server had taken their orders. Forrest had convinced them to skip the grilling until another day and to go out to eat instead.

"What do you mean?" Forrest asked, busying himself with getting Violet settled in the high chair. His mom was doing the same with Ivy.

"Well, your daughters were pretty excited to see Madeline, but you pretty much hurried them away from your bestie," Rosie added.

His parents were way too perceptive. "Okay, Mom, please don't use words like *bestie*, that's just weird. But to answer your question, Madeline was with her friend, and I didn't want the girls being a nuisance or disturbing her, so after they said a quick hello, I brought them to our table." That was such a lame excuse. When she'd said she had work stuff to do, he hadn't expected to run into her here or to feel a little miffed that she hadn't wanted to hang with him. Judging by the look on his parents' faces, they weren't buying it either. Madeline had been delighted to see his daughters, scooting over to make room for them. Holly'd had a full-wattage grin on her face, too, and she had appeared happy to see him. So, the girls had been anything but a nuisance.

"Okay. If that makes you sleep better at night," his father said, then smirked. "Although, I suspect you haven't been getting much of that *good* sleep."

His mother placed a hand over her mouth and tittered. "Duke, you need to behave yourself."

"You really gonna do me like that, Dad?" Forrest muttered.

The server returned with samples of chocolate-filled croissants and small plates. Duke placed a sample on each of their plates. His mother wagged her finger. "None for you."

"We'll go half and I'll give some to the girls." At her nod, he cut one in two, giving himself the bigger half. Then he jutted his jaw toward Madeline. "You really not going to fess up about what's going on with you two? I see you sneaking glances her way."

Busted. His face grew warm—his parents were making him feel like he was a snot-nosed sixteen-year-old again.

"He's blushing," Rosie laughed. But then her eyes grew serious. "Talk to us."

"I think I might have deeper feelings than friendship for Madeline," Forrest admitted, which wasn't true. He knew he did.

"That's great." She beamed. "I was worried after you and Cora that you had given up on relationships."

He popped a small piece of the croissant in Violet's mouth. Watching her eyes brighten and her mouth water made him laugh. "The attraction between us is off the charts, but that's how it was with Cora, too, and I just can't take the chance of things not working out, you know? I mean, when Cora and I split, the girls were too young to be affected by it. They don't remember the arguments or even that we once lived together. But now that they are older, they would be attached to Madeline, and I don't want to see them get hurt. Heck, *I* don't want to get hurt."

Duke rubbed his chin. "I get it. I do." Ivy held up her hands for him to pick her up. His father undid the seat belt and placed her on his lap. She immediately went for his entire piece of croissant. His father was now struggling to retract it from her fist.

Forrest wiped Violet's mouth and then continued. "Yeah, so though Madeline and I had a great night together, I decided that we needed to cool things off. Just be friends. It's easier that way—" He stopped mid-sentence. There was a guy at Madeline's table. Well-built. Solid. The dude seemed to be flirting with them and both women were eating it up. Jealousy swirled within him, especially since the man seemed to be writing on a small piece of paper. That meant he was giving out the digits and Madeline had slipped it inside her purse. However, being friends meant that she was free to flirt, to date, to do as she pleased.

He didn't like it.

"Easier doesn't mean better, son," his mother said, resting her hand over his, bringing his attention back to her.

"Tell me about it," he mumbled.

Madeline stood and bent over to get her purse, giving him a great view of her butt. Those two perfect globes he'd once cupped in his hands. A butt that dude definitely ogled before heading out the door.

A different kind of hunger brewed in his loins. She threw back her head, laughing at something Holly said, arching those plump breasts. He needed to look away, but he *couldn't.* At that precise moment, Madeline glanced his way. The look between them could best be defined as electric. The girls yelled for her, and she gave them a wave before leaving with Holly.

Suddenly, he felt hallow, like she had carried all the sunshine with her. However, he was soon distracted by some delicious smells. Their food had arrived.

Forrest had ordered fruit and oatmeal for the girls and chicken and waffles for himself. Just as he was taking out two sippy cups of milk from the baby bag, his cell pinged. It was Madeline.

Good running into you.

Likewise.

Talk soon?

Sure.

That short exchange gave him a boost. Madeline wasn't giving up on him—or their friendship—and a wave of relief went through him.

Duke gave Forrest's food a longing stare before sighing at the chicken omelet on his plate. But then Rosie reached over to plant a kiss on his cheek. "It's alright, love. Your omelet will be the best you've ever tasted." She reached into her purse and pulled out a bottle of hot sauce. "I brought this for you to have a little bit." Duke gave her a grateful look, and she responded with a gentle pat on his arm. "Just a small amount, okay?" Then she bit into her English muffin, which she had gotten with jelly, before taking a sip of her coffee.

Their exchanges made his heart melt. How did he get blessed with such loving parents? He poured syrup on his waffle and cut off a slice. It tasted delicious. One thing he had learned from having twin daughters was how to eat quickly, because once they finished their fruit, they would be ready for their oatmeal.

"Did I ever tell you about when your mother and I were dating?" Duke asked him.

"You've told me lots of stories, Dad."

Duke wiped his mouth. "I don't think I told you about how we almost broke up?"

His eyes went wide. "No. No, you didn't." He looked between them. "You two almost broke up?"

"Yes, because my heart was closed to love. I was living my best life as a bachelor and then this feisty little woman came along and knocked me off my feet. I was scared. I couldn't handle it."

His mother chimed in. "That's right. He couldn't."

Goose bumps popped up on his flesh. His father's experience was a direct echo of his own dilemma. "So, what happened?"

"I told her we had to go our separate ways. Didn't even give her a reason. But here's the kicker—Rosie didn't argue or even ask why. She simply said, 'If that's how you want it,' and then walked right out the door while my mouth hung open."

"Yup. I sure did." Rosie lifted her chin. "The way I saw it, if you had to think about being with me, you didn't deserve me."

Go, Mom. Forrest ran a finger down the bridge of his nose. Was that how Madeline felt?

"I was shook. Days went by and she refused to answer my calls. That's when I came to a realization, which changed things. If I didn't want the best thing in my life to slip away, I was going to have to conquer these fears and win her back."

"And I made him sweat, too," Rosie said, giving Forrest a knowing smile. "I didn't go running just because he came a calling. No, sir. He was going to have to convince me to give him another chance."

Shoot, his mother was a baddie. He was eating this up.

"Needless to say, she made me work for it. Took some time. But I eventually won her over," Duke told him.

"I love how it all worked out for you guys. But it's different for me. The stakes are higher because I have my girls to consider." The walls around his heart hardened.

"Hiding behind your girls is a copout." Duke reached over and rested a hand on his shoulder. "What are you really afraid of, son?"

"Being wrong about her the way I was wrong about Cora," he whispered hoarsely.

Rosie pointed at Ivy and Violet. "Good still came out of that relationship. She made you a father. Gave you these two precious girls. I'm sure you don't regret having them."

Not for a second. They were his air…his reasons to face another day. "I don't even remember what my life was like before them," he conceded. "Did I even have a life?" He dragged Violet's high chair closer and fed her some of the oatmeal since most of it had ended up on the table instead of her mouth. His mother did the same for Ivy.

"You did. All those rodeo awards are a testament to that. But your daughters grounded you. They gave you purpose."

"Perfectly stated, Dad."

His father pierced him with a stare. "So, again I ask, son, what are you really afraid of?"

After nighttime prayers, Forrest tucked his twins in bed and then kissed their foreheads. "I love you, Ivy. I love you, Violet. Have sweet sleep and good dreams."

Two sets of droopy eyelids; two sleepy I-love-yous and two yawns followed his words. He turned off the lights, the glow of the night-light filling the room. Leaning against the doorjamb, he watched as the girls finally gave in to sleep's call. His heart was a squishy ball.

Madeline should be here with him.

He straightened at that thought. That's right—she *should* be right here next to him, where she belonged, because he loved her. He was *in love* with Madeline Fortune. That realization stunned him. Frightened by the deluge of strong emotions hitting his system, Forrest immediately began the mental backtracking.

Maybe he wasn't in love and was just in need of a good night's sleep. What he was experiencing could be a combination of seeing her earlier, his girls' reactions, and his parents' love stories. He definitely needed to sleep on this before making any rash declarations. Once he was well rested, he might come to his senses.

Besides, he had been so adamant about preserving their friendship that it was probably best he left things be instead of inviting Madeline on that roller-coaster ride called love.

Chapter Eleven

It was close to midnight, and Holly sat on Madeline's living room couch yakking away during the chick flick with no signs of jetlag. Not that she had a problem with it because her friend had spent countless nights at her home, but considering that she had just gotten back from Italy, it seemed feasible that Holly would want to go home at some point.

Finally, Madeline could take it no more. "Girl, my eyes are burning me. I've got to get some sleep. What are you doing?"

"Um, I was hoping I could stay here for a day or a week?" Holly asked.

A week? Madeline frowned. "What's going on?"

Her friend gave her a sheepish look. "I gave up my apartment right before you surprised me with the Italy trip, and I haven't done any apartment hunting while I was away. Then I ended my internship and changed my ticket to leave earlier, but I figured I could crash on your couch until I figured things out."

Madeline rushed to sit next to her. That was so unlike Holly that she was now truly concerned. "Of course, you can stay with me—you don't have to ask. But you should have let me know so I could be ready for you." She cocked her head. "Are you okay?"

"Yes, I..." Tears welled in Holly's eyes. Madeline grabbed a few tissues from the coffee table and handed them to her. "Thanks. I'm spontaneous, but I'm not usually this rash."

"Talk to me."

"This is going to sound silly, but I've got to talk to someone." Holly wiped her eyes. "A couple days ago, I met the most wonderful man at a vegetable stand, and he convinced me to play hooky for a day."

Madeline's brows rose. "You skipped the internship with Chef Henri?" She wanted to get a thermometer and check Holly's temperature, because only illness would have made her do that.

She nodded. "No, of course not. I was there for most of it. I just missed the last few days. So, this man and I went on this day-long escapade where he wined and dined me. He literally swept me off my feet." She touched her chest. "It was such a romantic day that I fancied myself in love with him."

"After *one* day?" The very idea was preposterous.

"Yep. I knew within the hour that I would spend the rest of my life with him if he would have me." Um, her friend had to be ill. Madeline placed her hand on Holly's forehead, but it was cool to the touch. She hiccupped. "But after one incredible night, I woke up the next morning in a five-star hotel and he was gone."

"Gone? Gone where?"

Holly lifted her shoulders. "I have no idea." She slipped a hand into her purse and pulled out a note. "For a second, I thought that I had imagined the whole thing, but then I found this note on the bathroom mirror." She held it open and read. "'Thank you. I'll never forget you. D.M.'"

"What does D.M. stand for?"

"I don't know."

Madeline blinked a few times as she processed those words. "Wait a minute. You went traipsing all over Italy and then ended up in bed with a man you only know as D.M.?" Please, Lord. Let her not have heard right.

"Yes." Her eyes filled. "That's why I didn't want to tell you at first. I'm so ashamed, but at the time, I was on this adventure. We both agreed to remain incognito, picking out code names." Her cheeks reddened. "He was Hammer and I was Evergreen."

"Hammer? Evergreen?" Madeline snickered.

"I was coming up with something on the fly. That's what I thought of," Holly said defensively. "And he was Hammer, because...well, you know..."

"Alrighty then. I'll leave that one alone." Madeline gestured with her hand. "Carry on with the story."

"I didn't know I would fall in love." She clutched her chest as her shoulders shook. "I didn't know he would break my heart as well."

Fall in love in a day? Geez. Was that even possible? Madeline bit back the words of disbelief. She could understand the one-night stand, but to experience heartache over a man Holly obviously didn't know was on a whole next level that made Madeline want to chew her bestie out for not using her good sense. Then again, Madeline had done the same with Forrest, but at least she knew him.

Actually, what did it matter if it was hours or months? Matters of the heart weren't bound by time constraints.

Her friend was suffering. She drew Holly in for a hug and rubbed her back. "I'm sorry you're hurting."

"We never exchanged phone numbers or contact information, but I asked the front desk about him. I searched and searched for him, visiting all the places we went together in hopes I would run into him, but it was like he had disappeared."

This D.M. sounded like a scam artist. Her friend might have been catfished. Madeline held Holly's shoulders. "Have you checked your phone or bank accounts for any suspicious activities?"

"Yes. All is as it should be. I wish he had done something because at least I would have a means to find him. I don't know how I'm supposed to go back to being normal after an encounter like this." Holly cried in earnest then. Big, ugly cry. Dang, this girl was about to make Madeline believe in love at first sight. Spent, Holly leaned back to ask, "Do you think I should hire a private investigator?" She answered her own question. "But I wouldn't even know where to tell him to begin." Another floodgate ensued. She knew Holly was a romantic, and that her friend felt things deeply, but her friend's reckless behavior had caught her off guard.

She offered words of comfort, but the thought most prevalent in her mind was that Holly seemed to have gone all out for a man she'd just met.

Meanwhile, Madeline had pretty much given up on a romantic relationship with Forrest—a man she knew intimately. A man she considered one of her best friends. Even if she didn't understand it, she could respect Holly's willingness to be so open and unguarded with her feelings.

Turning to her friend, she blew out a breath. "Well, I guess there's only one thing left to do..."

Holly smiled through her tears. "Bake cake." She stood and held out a hand.

Madeline got to her feet. "Exactly." Whenever they were stressed, cake was their pick-me-up. Holly had been the one to first suggest it when Madeline was going through the breakup with Ethan. They had prepared a batch of different kinds. It was methodical and therapeutic and delicious. And most of the time, they would think of a solution for their situation. If they didn't, then who cared? At least their stomachs were happy with cake.

Without another word, Madeline and Holly headed into her kitchen and Holly gathered the ingredients while Madeline retrieved the stand mixer, stainless-steel bowls and the KitchenAid.

It was twenty minutes before Holly voiced, "I should have gotten his name."

"You think?"

A second passed before Madeline snickered. Then Holly chuckled. Before they knew it, the friends were bowled over with laughter. Madeline's laughter mingled with relief. In time, her best friend was going to be just fine, and she would be too.

He was running through a field of sunflowers, holding Madeline's hand, when he heard it.

A loud, *demanding* cry.

At first, the sound seemed far away, but the more they ran in the direction of the sun, the louder the sound became. In a flash, Forrest was jolted awake into darkness, alone in his bed. There was that wail again.

He scampered out of bed and dashed into the twins' room. Turning on the light, he saw both twins sitting up in their toddler bed. However, it was Ivy who was crying. Her cheeks were splotchy, her face stained with tears. How long had his baby girl been crying? He went to pick her up and gasped.

She was burning up.

Forrest rushed to the bathroom to grab the thermometer out of the medicine cabinet. Then he placed it under her tongue and waited for the beep: *104 degrees*. That was too high. He had to get to the ER. He felt a pair of arms wrap around his leg. Violet wanted to be picked up.

"Hang on, baby. Daddy's got to take care of your sister first." Violet's little face fell. Then she, too, began to cry. He ran into the room to put on Ivy's shoes with Violet trailing behind him, begging him to pick her up. Goodness. He could feel the heat through Ivy's skin. He had to get to the hospital.

"I want Maddie," Ivy cried. Violet was now prostrate on the floor, her chest heaving. He was too overwhelmed with Ivy to correct Violet.

"Mommy isn't here," he said, hugging her close.

"Nooo. I want Maddie," the toddler sobbed, kicking her feet. He glanced at the clock. It was close to 2:00 a.m. Madeline was most likely asleep but he knew she would be okay with her reaching out to him. Putting the phone on speaker, he then worked on getting Violet's shoes on, which wasn't easy considering that she had stiffened her body.

"Behave, Violet. We have to go bye-bye."

There was a soft click, then Madeline's voice came through. "Forrest?" she asked.

Both girls were crying in earnest. "Hey, Madeline. I'm sorry to be calling you so late, but I've got a situation here and I desperately need your help. Ivy has a high fever, and I've got to get her to the ER, but she's been asking for you."

"We're on our way."

We?

"Hurry."

Fifteen minutes later, he had gotten both girls calmed enough to stop crying. Well, he had bribed them with ice pops, but they weren't letting him out of their sight. He opened the door to see both Madeline and Holly. Oh, that explained the "we." He sniffed. They smelled of vanilla, and if he wasn't mistaken, there were hints of frosting on their cheeks and hair.

The minute Ivy saw Madeline, she stretched her hands toward her and cried.

Madeline held her close, planting tiny kisses in her hair. "You'll be alright, sweetheart."

Low-key, Forrest wished she would do the same for him. It twisted up his insides seeing his daughter in distress. When either of his girls got sick, it was akin to kryptonite. He felt powerless. Thankfully, Madeline took charge, saying that Holly would stay with Violet while they went to the ER.

He sat in the back with Ivy while she drove at top speed.

"Thank you for coming," he croaked.

"No need to thank me. I'll always be there for you and your girls, no matter what."

The minute they entered the hospital and checked in at the reception desk, Ivy was taken back to be seen. A couple of hours later, they exited the ER, exhausted but relieved. Following a battery of tests, the physicians concluded that she had a virus that had to run its course. They advised Forrest to keep her hydrated and to use over-the-counter medication for fever management.

On the way home, Forrest took the driver's seat. Madeline sat behind him with Ivy. Seeing his baby girl's head lolling in her car seat reminded him that he wasn't the only one who was affected by Madeline's presence—or absence—in their lives. His daughters had grown quite attached and missed her just as much as he did when she wasn't around.

He pulled into the driveway, and Holly opened the front door and asked about Ivy.

"She will be fine. They think it's just a weird bug or something," Forrest said, opening the passenger door for Madeline. The eighteen-month-old clung to her, so he reached for the baby bag. "Thank you so much, Holly, for staying with Violet. I hope she wasn't much trouble."

"Not at all. She cried a little and went back to sleep. This was an easy gig." She yawned.

"Thanks, friend," Madeline said. "I appreciate you." She moved to hand Ivy off to him, but the child tucked her body into Madeline.

"I want you," she insisted, curling her fist around Madeline's shirt. Madeline gave him a hopeless look while rubbing Ivy's back.

"You can stay if you want," Forrest said.

With a nod, Madeline told Holly she would see her later. She then followed him inside and upstairs to the girls' room. Madeline rocked Ivy and sang her lullabies. She was so patient and tender, which just warmed his soul.

Madeline was a special woman, and his daughters recognized it. A whole bunch of emotions engulfed him—tenderness, gratitude…*desire*. He didn't know if he was just caught up in the moment, but all he could think about was the last time she was in his arms.

In his bed.

Once Ivy was asleep, Madeline came over to where he stood. She tilted her head back and smiled up at him.

"Thank you for tonight," he whispered. "I would have been lost without you." Then, because he *had* to touch her, he ran his fingers through her hair.

"You would have managed, but once again, you're welcome." She caressed his cheek. "We're always better together."

Those words pulled his gaze to her lips. He wrapped his arms around her, drawing her into him. Attraction coiled around them as the tension between them rose. His eyes dipped to her rising and falling chest, and then she licked her lips. His breath quickened. He had to taste her.

Forrest lowered his head. She closed her eyes and stood on tiptoes. The minute their lips connected, their passion exploded. There were moans and groans as his body molded itself to hers. Lord, she tasted sweet, and he had forgotten just how luscious her lips were. And she was giving as much as she was taking, which drove him crazy. Forrest felt like a hungry man who had just been fed after not eating for days. Her hands roamed his back, and he reached up to unhook her bra.

The light snap in the quiet was more like a boom, a crescendo. A heavy dose of reality. He was becoming consumed by her and that gave him pause.

Forrest tore himself out of her arms and backed up.

His chest heaved. "I'm sorry, I know it might seem as if I'm intentionally sending off mixed signals, but we can't do this. I value our friendship and don't want to jeopardize that. Plus, Ivy and Violet adore you. If we weren't to work out…"

A part of him wanted her to argue with him, tell him how wrong he was, but Madeline didn't do that.

She stepped back, her eyes tortured. "I can't be the only one fighting to give us a chance as a couple. If you want to be friends, fine, we'll just be friends. But keep your lips and hands to yourself. Stop looking at me like you want to devour me and quit giving anybody the evil eye who talks to me."

"You saw that?" Forrest didn't even bother pretending that he hadn't scowled at Dude from across the restaurant.

"I sure did." She shook her head and exhaled. "I'm tired of this yo-yoing back and forth. This is the last time I'm allowing myself to be put in this position with you. I'll reach out to check on Ivy tomorrow, *friend*. I'll catch an Uber home."

Gathering her stuff, she pulled up the Uber app and left him standing there.

Chapter Twelve

Croissants and crepes. It was barely past 7:00 a.m., but Holly had already made the delectable treats for breakfast. Madeline's stomach growled at the scintillating aromas.

"I'm still on European time," she said with way too much energy for the hour of the day. Holly was already dressed in a yellow-and-white maxi along with some sandals. Madeline was still in her pajamas and fuzzy slippers. "I've been dying for you to get up so you can dish how it went with Forrest once I left." She gyrated her hips. "Did you two do the tango?"

Madeline held up a hand. "Okay, I'm going to need you to never do that again." Helping herself to a croissant, she plopped onto one of the chairs around the dinette. That's when she noticed the small bouquet in a tiny glass bowl. "When did you get these?"

"ER Grocery had a few on display. I think they brighten up the space." She placed a crepe on her plate and poured them both a glass of orange juice.

"To answer your question. At most, there was a two-step before a toe-curling kiss then he—" she pulled up air quotes "—'came to his senses' and remembered we are just friends."

"Ugh. Forrest needs to quit playing with your emotions," Holly said, using her fork to move her crepe from one end of her plate to the next.

Madeline's brows rose. "Wait. Yesterday, you were gung-ho about my fighting for true love. What happened?"

Holly's shoulders slumped. "I found D.M."

She scooted to the edge of her seat. "What! Where? When?"

"His name is Dante Martinelli. His face was all over the newsstands when I went to ER Grocery."

Madeline's mouth dropped open. "He's famous?"

Holly rolled her eyes. "Yeah. Whatever. Apparently, he's some famous rock star who is gaining crossover appeal here in the US. I feel like he deceived me."

"Did he, though? Neither of you identified yourselves."

"Whose side are you on?" Holly asked, sounding disgruntled.

Instead of answering, Madeline strolled into her bedroom to grab her phone off the nightstand. Then she googled Dante Martinelli. She sucked in a breath at his picture. He was *supermodel fine.* Chiseled. She scurried into the kitchen and held up her phone so Holly could see the photo. "A man like this attracts attention wherever he goes. How did he escape notice?"

"He wore sunglasses and a cap for most of the day." Holly pointed to the food on Madeline's plate. "Don't let that go to waste." She took out a pastry box. "I'll take the rest to our office."

The words *our office* made her smile. "That's a great idea." Madeline took another bite, though her stomach was full from the gossip. "Are you going to reach out to him?"

Holly shook her head. "No. Nope. Never."

"I think you should."

A brow arched. "Pot. Kettle?"

"My case is different. I have tried a few times, and Forrest won't budge."

"Hmm… I see your point. I'll give it some thought, but for now, let's focus on work. Do we have anything on the schedule today?"

"Yes, we are meeting with another potential client. She wants to throw a divorce party." That was her first time receiving an inquiry through her website. Hiring a web designer had been worth the additional expense because if she landed this gig, she would recoup her investment and then some.

Holly's eyes went wide. "A *divorce* party?"

"Yes, she's celebrating a fresh start." Madeline glanced at her watch. "Sue is supposed to come to meet with us at 10:00 a.m., let's leave within the hour so I can grab paper goods and coffee pods for the office." She wasn't the best at making coffee, but she was fortunate to have the Coffee Connection close, and that would serve as her backup plan.

"Ooh, I can't wait to see what you've done to the place in person. Over the phone is nice, but you can't feel the ambience, the general vibe." Holly reached for another croissant as Madeline rushed off to get dressed.

The first thing that Madeline noticed when they entered ER Grocery was that it smelled of fresh linen. She made a note to grab a couple of diffusers for her office space. Pride filled her chest at having a space of her own for her business, which proved that her move to Emerald

Ridge had been fortuitous. A few months ago, she hadn't foreseen that she would accomplish this much.

She snatched up the last cart by the entrance. The store was jam-packed with customers and there was a long checkout queue. She prayed that they didn't venture into the 10 Items and Under line.

"I'm going to look at the plants while you get the coffee pods. We need to spruce up the place." Madeline was about to tell Holly that she already had plants, but she noticed her friend was making her way toward the magazines and books. She bit back a smile. Holly was probably going to see if she found more articles on Dante, but Madeline wouldn't call her out on it. She knew all about the need to feed the heart even when it made no sense. She had spent more time than she should have rereading her texts with Forrest, second-guessing if how she had answered had been the wisest move.

She rubbed her temples and weaved her way through the aisles. Love came with angst and complications, which made her head and heart hurt. She made quick work of gathering her items and then met up with Holly at the register, ignoring the trash mag tucked under her arm.

Afterward, she took her friend to Let's Get This Party Started, where Holly oohed and aahed over their establishment, high-fiving Madeline at least five times. Then she closeted herself in her office, presumably to bond with her new environment, but Madeline was pretty sure Holly intended to read the front-page spread on Dante.

Ten minutes before the divorcee's appointment, there was a rap on the door, and a courier entered, holding a card-sized envelope. "Ms. Madeline Fortune?" he asked.

She nodded. "Yes?"

"I have a package for you," he said, handing her the envelope.

"If you could sign here..." She complied, but the young man exited before she could ask who it was from.

Then she saw the fancy embossed script on the back of the envelope: *Susannah Simmons*. Her heart thundered and her hands shook as she carefully opened the lip. She pulled out a handwritten note.

Please respect my privacy. Thank you. S.

That's it?

Madeline flipped the card. The back was blank. Turning it over, she read the note again. And again. Dejection dueled with frustration in her chest as she clutched the note. Tears of frustration welled. She squeezed her eyes shut to keep them from falling.

Madeline rapped on Holly's door before entering, the overwhelming emotions engulfing her.

Her bestie slipped the magazine under her computer keyboard, dabbed at her eyes, then jumped to her feet. She rushed to Madeline's side and put an arm around her shoulder. "What's wrong?"

Madeline saw that Holly was distressed herself. "It's alright. I don't want to burden you. I know you have a lot on your mind..."

"A burden is easier to bear if two people are carrying it," Holly countered. "Tell me what's wrong."

"How did I luck out with such a best friend?"

"By being one yourself." Holly gave her a look of tenderness that soothed her soul.

"Dang, you have the best comebacks." Madeline waved

the envelope the way one would a flag in surrender and croaked out, "I've let Kate down. I've let her down *big-time*."

"Let me see." Taking the note, Holly read it before asking, "Susannah's not coming?"

"It doesn't look like it. She doesn't want to be bothered with any of us." The tears fell then as disappointment the size of bricks lined her stomach walls. "It was the one thing Kate asked me to do, and she had such faith in me." She hiccupped. "Without Susannah's presence, I might as well give up on this gala. My business is going to fold again."

"Whoa. You'll do *no* such thing."

"I don't have a choice." She shook her head. "This is going to be another scandal from which I'll never recover."

Holly lifted Madeline's chin using her index finger. Once Madeline met her eyes, she advised gently, "Don't say anything to Kate. Not just yet."

"Why not? It's better if I prepare her now. Waiting will make it harder."

"I get it. But sometimes, before you make a move, you have to sit in your feelings. You have to give your mind time to process, to accept, before you act."

Madeline wiped her tears. "What am I supposed to do in the meantime?"

"Continue planning and give Kate the biggest, baddest celebration Emerald Ridge has ever seen. A happy heart can forgive plenty."

She clung to Holly's wisdom. "Alright. I'll hold off for now…"

Holly wrapped her hands around Madeline's arms.

"Now, you listen to me. You have been busy nonstop lately and it's time to give yourself a break. Go do something wild, something adventurous—or treat yourself to a pedicure at The Style Lounge. I'm pretty sure Sophia will fit you in. Take care of *you* right now. I'll see to our client."

"But I need to be here. We need the business—"

"No, ma'am. What you need to do is trust me. I won't mess this up. It's a preliminary meeting, and I'll call if I'm in over my head." Then she shooed Madeline out the door.

"Are you sure?" Madeline put her foot in the doorjamb.

"Positive."

"But I don't know what to do."

"Do what you love." Holly folded her arms, stared her down until she removed her foot. Then her friend shut the door.

Temperance was missing.

With the irrigation resolved and all the inspections completed on his plot of land in Houston, Forrest was ready to conclude the sale of that property with a huge profit. He had been about to start his drive to Houston when Whitt called, frantic. His employee had just returned from lunch and noticed that the mare was missing.

Whitt was sure he had left her in the stall before his lunch break. None of the other ranch hands he had asked had any clue of what could have transpired. Nothing appeared amiss. So, how had she escaped? A tiny raindrop hit Forrest's arm. A peek up at the sky showed dark rain clouds. It was about to pour. He had to find Temperance before then.

"Saddle up Samson. I'll ride out to the edge of the

property. She couldn't have gone far." Taking Samson with him might make Temperance more docile to return home. He worried, though, that she might have gotten hurt.

"By the look and sound of it, we are going to get at least two inches of rain. Are you sure you want to venture out with Samson?" Whitt asked.

"I have to go." The man nodded and scuttled off to do his bidding. Forrest knew he should take the trailer instead. He didn't want to put Samson in danger, but his horse could go places where his truck could not.

Forrest couldn't imagine breaking the news to Madeline that her beloved mare was lost. *Madeline!* He needed to contact her and let her know what was going on. Tugging his phone out of his pocket, he gave her a quick call.

She answered on the second ring. "Hey, I was on my way back when Temperance got spooked by a clap of thunder. She took off, and I had a hard time getting her to calm down."

"*Back?*" He registered the sound of hooves and what sounded like rain.

"Yeah. I took Temperance out for a ride on the western edge of the property. Where we went before."

"You took…" He raked a hand through his hair and exhaled. "And you didn't think to tell anyone?" he asked, his tone gruff. He called out to Whitt to head home and notify the other staff.

"I didn't think I needed permission to ride my own horse."

"You don't. But I thought she escaped. You should have let someone know you were taking her out." He heard a huge boom followed by a downpour.

“I didn’t see—” she yelled.

He struggled to hear her through the storm. “See what?” He heard crackling but couldn’t decipher her words. Lightning flashed, striking the light. The barn was now covered in darkness. He thought he heard a yelp and cupped the phone to his ear. “If you can hear me, go find shelter,” he commanded, praying she understood his warning. But the line went dead. Forrest’s stomach knotted. The thought of Madeline out there on her own, braving the elements with a skittish horse, made his knees weaken.

Pacing the barn, he told himself that Madeline was an experienced horsewoman. She would know to wait out the storm and to keep Temperance calm.

Forrest called Junie to check on her and the girls. His sitter told him the main house had electricity and his daughters were playing, unfazed by the weather. Good. He let Junie know his plans to search for Madeline and her horse.

Beside the barn door was a rack that held ponchos. He grabbed two, one for himself and another for Madeline. He dashed outside, intending to hitch the horse trailer to his truck, but Whitt had already done it. Gratitude flowed through his veins.

“I got you, boss,” Whitt said, ignoring how the rain poured through his locks.

“Thank you. You’re the best,” Forrest said.

“Do you need me to tag along?”

“No. I want you to get home and out of this weather.” Whitt had arthritis and it had to be acting up with all this rain.

“Okay. Be safe out there.”

It was really coming down now. He drove with limited visibility, but Forrest knew his land. His worry for Madeline and her horse skyrocketed when he saw how muddy it was. They both could be in danger. But he knew one thing—if it took him all night, he wasn't going to stop looking until he found them.

Madeline wasn't even sure if she was still on Forrest's property. She had found an abandoned, dilapidated shed to wait out the storm and had harnessed Temperance to the rotting post outside the door. Since there was an overhang, though tattered, Madeline and the horse were somewhat shielded from the downpour. The shed was at the end of a graveled path, tucked away from the main road, which she had followed to this location.

She had tucked a couple of apples in the saddle sack before leaving, so she gave one to the horse and she nibbled on another.

"I'm sorry I took you out in this, Temperance," Madeline said, shivering in her wet clothes. "As soon as the rain lets up, we will head back to warmth and safety." She had been out here for close to two hours. The horse whinnied and rubbed its nose along her arm. She was so thankful that Temperance was proving to be a loyal friend, because right now she needed one.

Her cell phone had no signal and had only an eight percent charge, so she avoided making any calls. But she had sent her location to Forrest, hoping he had received it. She was saving whatever power she had left for when Forrest found her. If she knew her friend, he was looking for her. That's why she had decided to stop here instead of trekking in the dark. It was best she remained in one spot, which would make it easier for him to locate.

Madeline snapped her fingers. *Fire.* She needed to start a fire. The smoke could serve as a beacon if this shed had a fireplace. Using the light on her phone, she crept up the stairs, holding on to the rail, acutely aware that the structure itself leaned to the right. A strong, musty odor assailed her. She walked toward the fireplace, the wood soft and spongy under her feet. If she tried to kindle a fire, the whole thing would go up in flames.

Plus, there were bugs and overgrown vegetation on the inside.

Whew. Maybe she was safer outside.

Turning around, she went to sit on the top of the steps, praying the foundation wouldn't cave. She wiped her brow. The rain had tapered some, but now it was muggy. She felt grimy and hot and alone.

As if she had read her mind, Temperance snorted as if to say, *I'm here*.

"Yes, you are, girl." She stroked the mare's mane, feeling comforted. That's when she heard a faint honk and a voice, she knew very well calling her name. Madeline spun around and called out to the man she loved—her rescuer. "Forrest!"

Another honk.

Then lights. *Lights!*

Adrenaline surged through her body. Madeline trudged through the mud toward the brightness, yelling, "Forrest!"

She heard a faint, "Madeline!"

"Over here." Her knees weakened. He had found her. She waved and waved. The vehicle stopped a few feet away from her, the only sound the squishing of the windshield wipers. Then a creak as the driver's door cracked open and a boot, a lean, strong body, and an achingly familiar face came into view.

Madeline moved as fast as her legs could carry her toward him. His legs ate up the distance between them—and the next thing she knew, Forrest scooped her into his arms, holding her tight.

"Thank God, I found you. I was so worried. I would have never forgiven myself if something happened to you and I didn't get the chance to—" He stopped and squeezed her tight. "I'm just glad I found you."

She clung to him, her hands gripping the back of his head. "I knew you would come for me." She hiccupped. "How did you find me? Did you get the location ping I sent you?"

"No. I chose a path I didn't normally go."

Those words were her undoing. The dam to her tears burst free, and her body convulsed under the gravity of her emotions.

"Shh…it's okay. I got you." Forrest held her against his chest, grounding her; his heartbeat an anchor.

He slid inside the truck, pushing the seat back, without releasing her. She cried until she was spent. Then a new awareness arose.

Madeline planted kisses of gratitude along his neck. His hands tightened on her butt. Desire flickered to life. Their lips met, and with every ragged breath and scorching touch, they surrendered to the passion that refused to be banked. Soon she straddled him, his hands in her hair, his groans echoing throughout the confines of his truck. His sexy sounds fanned her hunger, her only thought to assuage the demands of her body.

But then she thought of his wishy-washy behavior, and Temperance, and common sense pierced through the sensual haze. She scooted off his lap. "As much as I would love to, we've got to get Temperance back to the barn."

"You're right." Forrest gave her a look of regret and longing before touching her cheek. "I'll be right back. Stay put. Warm up."

She nodded and turned up the heat while Forrest tended to Temperance and put her in the trailer.

During the drive back to Forrest's ranch, neither of them spoke. Madeline's eyes became heavy, and he seemed lost in his thoughts. She must have drifted off because the next thing she heard was a screech from a voice she recognized.

"This can't be true. It can't be. Please don't tell me that you were the one who bought this horse from right under me!"

Chapter Thirteen

Forrest froze at Cora's voice. "What are you doing here?" he asked in a low voice, carefully leading the mare out of the trailer. Madeline was still asleep inside the truck, and if he were lucky, she would stay that way until he could get rid of his ex.

"My plans got derailed because of the weather. There was a tornado watch in the path of the railway, so our trip was postponed until tomorrow. I came by to see the girls for a little bit, but they were already in bed," Cora rushed to say, then pointed to Temperance. "But back to my original question. How did you come to own this particular horse?"

"I purchased a piece of land, and the owner offered it to me. I couldn't say no." He traipsed into the barn. *Please don't let her follow me.*

But she was right on his tail. "Dean and I drove all the way to Houston for this very horse." Something in her intonation angered Temperance. She kicked her hind legs. Fortunately, Cora moved quickly enough to avoid getting hurt.

He lifted his shoulders. "Cora, what do you expect me to do about this now? That is all water under the bridge." Though he spoke with finality, his heart galloped inside his chest. Forrest led Temperance into her stall, and Samson walked over to nuzzle the mare.

She frowned. “Let me buy her off you. You don’t know how badly I wanted this horse.”

“Can’t.”

“Can’t or *won’t*?” She pushed.

“He can’t give away what doesn’t belong to him. The horse is mine.” Madeline’s voice rang out from behind them. Cora spun around to see her standing by the barn door. He could’ve used a thunder roll or some other kind of divine intervention, but all was quiet. “Temperance was a gift from Forrest to me. She lives here, but she belongs to me.”

“You bought her a horse?”

Madeline placed a hand on her hip. “Yes, he did. You don’t have to talk about me like I’m not here.”

Cora gave her a scathing side glance before pinning her eyes on Forrest and asking her question again.

Forrest squared his shoulders and nodded. Cora flailed her hands, startling both horses. “Take it easy,” he cautioned. “I don’t want them agitated.”

Madeline ambled over to the horses to comfort them, leaving Forrest to finish the conversation with Cora. She probably figured they were much better company. Wise woman.

Cora drew in a deep breath and took a few seconds to compose herself. “Please accept my apology.” She massaged her temples. “I was caught off guard. It’s your business how you spend your money and whom you spend it on. It’s just that I had really wanted that horse.”

“Why?” Forrest asked, his tone softening.

"She's beautiful and a challenge," Cora said. "A chance to prove to myself that I can manage a powerful horse."

"It's okay not to be good at everything, you know."

Her shoulders slumped. "I know…"

"Have you ridden the horse that Dean bought you as yet?"

"A couple of times." She scrunched her nose. "The poor dear is a constant pooper. It's quite the turnoff."

He chuckled. "It comes with the territory."

"If I'm being honest, I think I need a different hobby." She then walked over to Madeline to apologize for her curtness. The horses put up a fuss at her presence, but she didn't freak out, which was progress. The women hugged it out briefly before she waved at him and left.

Madeline sauntered over. "She thanked me for loving her daughters and says she's glad I'm in their lives."

"That was sweet. Cora doesn't say anything she doesn't mean."

"Well, that's something we have in common." She covered a yawn. "I'd better be going. I have a long day tomorrow."

Suddenly, Forrest didn't want her to leave, not relishing the thought of being alone in that big bed, especially since he was still turned on after their makeout session in his truck. He touched her arm. "Don't go. Stay the night with me." His chest heaved while he waited for her response.

Madeline stared at him, chewed on her lip, before she stepped back and shook her head. "If it's alright with you, I'm going to pass. Like I told you before, I'm done with all this back and forth. I can't function like that, and I don't want to go to bed happy and wake up to uncertainty. We have all this chemistry between us, but I can't go on this journey with you without a clear indication of where we're going. That isn't fair to either one of us. I think we need to take a step back from all of that and stay focused on our friendship. Understand?"

He nodded. Though her rejection pinched like a clamp to his heart, he had been as fickle as the weather. But that was all before she went missing. That made him realize just how much he loved her. Forrest wanted to tell Madeline that, but that could be misconstrued as manipulation.

No, it was best he let her leave and save that revelation for a more appropriate time.

"I completely understand." He squeezed the words out, contenting himself with hugging her and watching the sway of her hips as she walked away. He had a premonition that that was the beginning of the end of their friendship, and he had no idea how he would even begin to cope with that.

"Whoa. It sounds like you had quite the adventure last night," Holly said to Madeline the next morning as they entered the storefront. By the time Madeline had gotten into her condo, Holly had already been asleep. She had tossed and turned most of the night, questioning her decision to resist Forrest's tempting proposal. Because her body had been upset with her. However, once she had recounted everything to Holly, her best friend had agreed with her, saying that Forrest needed to get a taste of his own medicine.

"I don't know if I would call it an *adventure*," Madeline said, her voice sounding gravelly. "I was feeling pretty defeated after Susannah sent that note, and all I wanted to do was ride Temperance and escape. I didn't foresee that I would get stranded in one of the worst storms we've had this year."

Holly went around the office, turning on the lights before starting up the Keurig. "Well, the main thing is that you made it through, and Forrest got to play a real-life hero."

Unlike Madeline, who had darkened circles around her eyes, and had dragged on a pair of jeans and at T-shirt before tucking her hair under a cap, Holly looked refreshed in her floral dress and white sandals. Madeline had already told her bestie that she would be the front woman in charge today. She needed recovery time.

Besides, she had a behind-the-scenes task to complete.

Madeline had set an appointment with the same web designer who had done her website to create a special 100th birthday website for Kate. She planned to have more family members learn about Kate's history and also post comments and pictures. Madeline believed that she would appreciate this gesture and it would be a balm, especially since it seemed like Susannah was going to be a no-show.

"How did it go with our new client yesterday?" Madeline asked.

"It went better than expected. Turns out she's the first of four friends to get divorced and she plans to recommend us for when they throw their parties."

"That's a downer. I don't know if I wanted to be branded for that."

"Well, cash is cash," Holly countered. "She asked for our business cards or a brochure of what we offer, but I had to direct her to our website."

"I put the order in a couple of days ago at the print shop

down the block. They said it would be ready sometime this morning. I'll head down there." Madeline watched the drip-drop of the coffee like a horse feigning for a carrot. She was claiming that first mug.

"Hey, I've been thinking that since everybody in Emerald Ridge has been talking about Kate's party, that maybe we should host a teaser this weekend. Generate a bigger buzz."

Madeline quirked a brow. "What are you thinking?"

"What if we host a day at the park? It would give the vendors a chance to showcase what they plan to bring. And Susannah might hear about it and get curious..."

She rubbed the bridge of her nose. "That's a *genius* idea! Curiosity brings profit." Finally, the Keurig machine quieted, and Holly handed her a steaming mug. *Aww.* She was so kind. "Thank you, friend."

"No prob. You look like you need it." Holly placed another cup to brew. Madeline chuckled, keeping her snappy comeback to herself. After all, her friend was right. She needed this coffee to perk her up.

"Do you have the visitor list to send off the emails to your Fortune clan?" Holly asked.

"Yep. I'll generate the evite as soon as I finish my coffee." Madeline blew into her mug. "So, did you get in touch with D.M.?"

Holly's smile slipped. "I read through a lot of articles about him. Eventually, I found one where they had his publicist's contact information, and I reached out, but it is highly unlikely that it will pan out. So, I'm determined to not think about him anymore and to chalk my time with Dante up to the day I'll treasure for a lifetime."

"If he feels the same, he'll hunt the globe until he

finds you. But in the meantime, let's plan a divorce party and drum up some business."

An hour later, Madeline exited her storefront and walked across the street to the other building. A tall dude, whose face was hidden underneath a pair of dark shades and a baseball cap, held the door open for her. Thanking him, she stepped inside and greeted the owner, Brent. This space was even smaller than hers but boasted two printing presses, a few color copiers, a binding machine, computers, and a photo center.

Whenever she could, Madeline supported small enterprises, since she knew firsthand how your customer base could make or break your business.

"Your business cards are ready," he said. "We're almost finished packaging your posters. We had to reprint them because of the bleed. My son underestimated the cut on the edges." It was a two-man team, consisting of Brent and his teenaged son, Oscar. His wife died when Oscar was a baby and he'd been single ever since.

"No worries. Take your time." She pointed at the greeting cards. "I'll just go check these out while I wait."

There was a platter of large cellophane-wrapped oatmeal cookies on the counter. "Do me a favor and take one of those off my hands." Brent patted his waist. "Keeps me from ruining my lunch and preserving my waistline."

She chuckled and helped herself to one of the biggest ones on the plate and then sauntered toward the greeting cards. She glimpsed a familiar Stetson in the back of the store and saw her brother, Penn.

"Hey, sis." He waved. "What brings you here?"

"Just picking up some promo materials for my business. I finally moved into the storefront two doors down."

His green eyes flashed. "How exciting! I've got to pop in to check out your space."

"Family is welcome anytime." She loved how Penn's face lit up at those words. Madeline knew she was cheesing, too. It sure was nice not being an only child.

"How are things going with Kate's party planning?" he asked.

"Everything is going according to plan, except for Susannah Simmons, which is a bummer because Kate really believed in me. Last month, I wrote a letter to her and explained all about Kate and how much it would mean to her if Susannah showed up to her gala in July—"

"And did she respond?"

"Yeah, but it wasn't what I was hoping for. She had a courier deliver me a note." Madeline reached into her purse and pulled it out so he could read it.

"Don't let that get you down. Besides, if the town papers are true, then you're putting off the party of the century. Pun intended. I hear you're recreating a mini version of Cowboy Country USA."

"That is correct. The papers are not exaggerating. The amusement park is a project and a half, but so worth it. I know Kate is going to love that. There will be Fortunes from different branches in attendance to celebrate Kate—even those that are related to the royal family."

"Wow. That's impressive. You're pulling off a major feat. I'm so proud of you, Madeline."

"Yeah. It's what I do," she said, giving herself a pat on the back. The siblings laughed. Then she cocked her head. "Hey, did you get the evite I sent this morning?"

She had also sent Forrest an invitation, and though she hadn't received his response as yet, she knew her best friend would be there, despite the uncertainty of their relationship as a couple.

Penn's brow furrowed. "I don't think I got one… Let me check my email. Hopefully, it didn't go to my spam." He pulled out his phone. "Ah, here it is." With a few taps, he said, "There. I've accepted."

"Great. I invited Susannah as well to the Fortune Family Day, but I have no expectations for her presence after that note."

"Don't give up hope. If it's any consolation, I'm stoked to meet Kate Fortune. I read up on her and she's lived such an amazing life."

Madeline nodded. "I know, right? The one I find truly fascinating is that Kate survived a plane crash all by herself at age fifty. Did you read about that?"

"No." Penn's eyes widened. "I can't even imagine that."

"Well, I've compiled all the remarkable stories of her life and created a website. I'll send out the link soon. Family and friends will be able to leave their well wishes for Kate on her birthday. I think it is something she will treasure."

"I'm looking forward to meeting this phenomenal woman. I'm curious to know how Dad and Kate knew each other. There's so much about him I feel that I don't know."

"I have no idea," Madeline said. "But I know that he did reach out to Kate and recommended me planning her party. But I hope to find out their connection from Kate. When I asked her about it, she was quick to end the call, but I figure I'll ask her in person when I see her at the party this July."

"I like that plan," Penn said. "Keep me posted."

"Oh, you best believe I'll be posting all about it in our group chat," Madeline said.

Brent called out that her print order was ready. She had already paid online when she'd ordered, so all she had to do was pick up the boxes bearing her name. Penn insisted on carrying her packages despite her protest. But it also meant he had the chance to check out her storefront.

As she showed her brother her office space, she couldn't help but think how Forrest had yet to tour it. And after their exchange last night, he might not cross the threshold anytime soon. The knowledge that their friendship would probably transition into mere associates saddened her. But friends were in your life for a reason, a season, or a lifetime. And it appeared as if Forrest had been her friend for a season. Now, it was time to begin a new chapter. But how did she do so when she wasn't ready to turn the page just yet?

Chapter Fourteen

Whoever said misery loved company obviously didn't know Madeline or have a friend like Holly. Because Madeline very much wanted to be alone and burrowed deep under her covers, only putting on a happy face when dealing with clients or vendors. But Holly refused to let her do so.

Even though Holly was pining over her rock star, she was energetic, pouring all her emotions into baking all kinds of goodies, thus making Madeline feast on tarts, eclairs and chocolate mousse.

Seated behind her desk in her office, she bit into a warm cookie and groaned. Would the torture never end?

From the time she rolled out of bed in the morning and rolled back into bed at night, she was eating. Whenever she tried to bring up Forrest or Dante, Holly would hand her a dessert. Eat therapy over talk therapy was Holly's motto.

However, Madeline *wanted* to talk about Forrest because when she wasn't occupied with work, he and his girls filled her thoughts. She had spent the past hour looking at photos and reading through past text messages.

"Text me. Call me. Something." She slammed the

phone face down on her desk and took another bite of her cookie.

Madeline brought up the newly constructed website for Kate's 100th birthday. There were four pages: *All About Kate*, *Fortune Family Tree*, *Photos*, and *Tributes*. Each would always be a work in progress based on the continuous input from family and friends. Madeline didn't know which page was her favorite because the more she added, the more her love and admiration for this remarkable woman grew.

She especially loved reading *Tributes*. Kate's generosity had touched so many lives, including hers. The vast number of responses to this website had led her to hire the designer as the permanent webmaster to manage the content.

A notification flashed across her screen. It was a track shipment for the plushies she had ordered for the girls. Excited, Madeline clicked on the link. They were being shipped overnight from Tennessee, so she would have them tomorrow.

If Forrest and the girls showed up to the Fortune Family Day this weekend, she could give them to the twins then. But he had yet to respond to her invitation. And she had checked at least fifty times for a reply.

She could also just stop by his house and drop them off. That's something friends did; except she wasn't exactly sure of the status of their relationship. Madeline and Forrest were at a crossroads, each sitting at the stop sign, neither being the first to take their foot off the brake.

Pushing back her chair, Madeline picked up what was left of her cookie and traipsed out of her building to get some fresh air.

Holly was out shopping for dessert items, having volunteered to create pastries for this weekend. Madeline prayed Dante found Holly soon, or the town was going to be on a sugar high from her bestie's baking. People were popping into her storefront to grab a party planning postcard but, really, they wanted to get one of Holly's treats.

Madeline also had another purpose for coming outside. She strolled to the vacant storefront adjacent to hers and peered through the window. From the moment she'd seen the For Sale sign, Madeline had kept an eye out so she could talk with the owner. She had no business even considering expansion when she was starting over, but she had a vision.

With her best friend by her side, that vision could be a reality. This was a calculated risk worth taking. Seeing movement inside, Madeline rapped on the door. A burly man with receding red hair and a cheery countenance opened the door.

"What can I do for you?" he asked with an Irish lilt, wiping away the dust from his forehead and cheeks.

After greeting him, and learning his name was Artie, she asked, "I wanted to find out if this space was still available."

"It sure is. You want to come have a look-see."

"Yes, if I may." He stepped aside so she could enter. Her breath hitched. Since she had just renovated her space, Madeline hadn't had expansion in her plans. But her business was booming and she had two reliable workers. Besides, this was a good risk and, even without the tour, she knew she wanted it. She wanted to jump up and down like the twins, but she kept her tone casual. This was even more spacious than her own storefront. She couldn't risk him upping the price. "I'd love to see the rest, if I'm not interrupting."

"A sale is never an interruption," Artie quipped.

Madeline chucked. "That's a good one. I might have to use it."

"It's open source." Artie was quick with the comebacks. An indication of an astute businessman, perhaps. He took her through to the back room, which he said used to be a kitchen space, and there was storage in the back. When she heard that, she almost whooped. This was perfect for what she had in mind. Emerald Ridge already had three cafés, but there was always room for more, especially since this one would be specialized. The town was expanding daily, and the consumer demand was there. She dabbed at the perspiration on her forehead. It sure was hot, though.

"What's your asking price?" she breathed, unable to contain her excitement. He named a figure so low that her brows creased. "Did it pass all the necessary inspections?"

"Yep. There are no hidden damages, and I just upgraded the commercial kitchen and put new flooring in. I know I caught you off guard with that number, but I like you."

Madeline didn't think that was smart business, but the price was too sweet to pass up. She held out a hand. "I'll take it."

They shook hands. Then Artie confessed, "I saw your face when I said I liked you. You remind me of the daughter I lost three years back. And I wish I had supported her when she decided to break away from the family business. I was just thinking about that when you walked through the door. That's serendipity." His voice broke. "I see you as my chance to make things right."

"Wow… I'm sorry for your loss. Having just lost my dad, I feel your pain." If he weren't a stranger, she would have hugged him.

"It's okay. I'd like to think she'd be proud of me." That's it—she *had* to hug him. There were such beautiful people in the world, and Artie was one of them. The fact that his name was so close to her father's had to mean something. Artie's chin wobbled, and he patted her on the back before letting go. "Thank you for stopping in. I'll get the paperwork to you and I'll be sure to get the AC up and running before then."

She strutted to the door feeling blessed to be a property owner. Madeline turned the knob and paused. "Listen, I know we just met, but I'd love it if you come to the Fortune Family Day I'm hosting this weekend at the amusement park."

His eyes went wide. "I've been hearing about that. Sure, I'd love to come. Are you sure it won't be an imposition? I don't want anybody looking at me sideways."

"Not at all. The more, the merrier."

"Alright. See you around noon to sign the paperwork."

Holly was in the reception area when she dipped back into their store. Madeline drew in a deep breath and splayed her hands. "Thank goodness for AC."

"Where were you?" Holly asked. "I came looking for you to talk lunch but also to share that we have three divorce parties booked."

"Woot! Woot!" Madeline did a jig. "That's great news because I just purchased the property next door."

"Say what?"

"Yes. I was thinking of expanding my party planning business by adding a patisserie." She gave Holly a pointed look. "And I know the perfect *partner* well versed in French pastries, if she's interested."

"Partner?" Holly's eyes flashed.

"Of course. You've invested all you had, and you're my ride or die. We're in this together and we're going to profit together."

Holly squealed and launched herself into Madeline's arms. The friends rocked back and forth. "I love you, bestie."

"Not as much as I love and appreciate you."

All of a sudden Holly froze and stepped back. "I was so excited I forgot to tell you the latest update." Madeline gestured for her to get to it. "Dante is on his way here to Emerald Ridge. His publicist reached out. He might even be here already."

Madeline's mouth dropped. "Yay. That is great news. I'm glad he knows a good woman when he finds one." She gasped and put a hand over her mouth. "Oh my goodness. I think he is already here. I think I saw Dante when I went to the print shop the other day. There was a guy with a baseball cap and shades leaving as I was going in, so I didn't get a good look at him, but it could have been Dante."

Holly shook her head. "I doubt it. That was days ago. Why wouldn't he have come to see me before then?"

"Yeah, maybe you're right," Madeline said. "Either way, Dante is coming to Emerald Ridge, and you'd better get camera ready because I'm sure he is going to set the town abuzz with his visit."

A camera flash made both women spin around.

* * *

His baby girls loved the water. That's why, since it was in the eighties and there was no forecast of rain, Forrest had jumped at his parents' invitation to bring the girls over for steaks and swimming. Right now, there were Porter cuts on the grill and beef brisket in the smoker, which his father was tending to, and his mother was in the pool with the girls.

Rosie had allowed his father a red meat day, and Duke was taking advantage of it.

Forrest also had a secret motive for coming over besides giving Rosie and Duke time with their grandbabies. Frankly put, his ears needed a break.

For the past few days, all he heard was Madeline. Madeline. Madeline.

Can Maddie come play?

I want Maddie!

Maddie this and Maddie that. No matter how he tried to distract them, they would bring her up. And all that served to do was add to his misery. Shoot, he wanted her, too, but he couldn't very well tell her that when this whole "friends only" stipulation had been *his* wish. He hadn't spoken to Madeline since the night of the storm and he was feeling every minute of it.

Stretched out on a pool lounger, Forrest was desperately trying not to show his desolation though. He had dressed in swim trunks, a white tee, and had slapped on a pair of sunglasses. He was the picture of unbothered. Too bad that was a lie.

Rosie waded over to him and angled her body so she could still see the girls sitting on the steps at the shallow end of the pool. She was dressed in a slimming black swimsuit and had on a straw hat to shield her from the sun. Forrest turned so he could see his girls. "Why don't you call Maddie and invite her over?"

If only his mother knew the number of times he had reached for his phone to do just that. But her words, *If it's alright with you, I'm going to pass*, kept replaying in his mind. When she'd uttered them, Forrest had gotten the impression she had been talking about more than spending the night in his bed. It felt like she was taking a break from him. He didn't know if that was for good or if she just needed time, but the fact that she hadn't texted or called was telling. To be fair, neither had he.

"She's busy planning Kate Fortune's birthday gala," he said to his mother, hoping Rosie would be satisfied with that answer. But she was not going to drop it.

She placed a hand on her hip. "Madeline has never been too busy for you. I think you're avoiding her."

"We're not avoiding each other. We made a choice." He slid off the lounger and moved in closer proximity to his daughters.

"So, this is what you wanted?"

Instead of answering that question, Forrest suggested they get out of the pool. He needed to reapply fresh sunscreen and check if the twins needed a diaper change. He scooped them under his arms and walked out of the water.

When the girls protested, his mother went into the shed and took out the kiddie pool. "I swear, your daughters are like fish. They would stay in the pool all day if you let them."

His father left the grill and turned on the outside hose to fill the large rubber tub. Forrest pressed the remote to close the pool while Rosie led the girls over to get into the kiddie pool. Seeing that their swim diapers were soaked, Forrest tore those off and put on new ones. Both girls' eyes drooped, and Violet let out a big yawn.

"I'm not sure the twins are going to need the kiddie pool," Forrest said. "I think they are ready for some much-needed rest."

"That's okay. This will be here if they want to play later. They are going to have a good nap after being in the sun," Duke said, sloshing across the lawn to turn off the spigot.

"I'll take them inside," Rosie offered.

Forrest's tummy led him to the grill. The steaks sizzled from the butter and herbs. "I'll take these off now to rest." He grabbed the tongs.

"Good idea." Duke plodded over to the smoker. When he opened it, Forrest's mouth watered from the tantalizing smell hitting his nostrils. His father used a fork to get a taste of the burnt ends. "This is so tender, it's melting in my mouth. Your mother put her foot in this homemade barbecue sauce."

Madeline loved beef brisket. Maybe he could take some to her for lunch. The girls were asleep and so he could dip out for an hour or so… Forrest scuttled into the kitchen and got a few containers for the salad, corn and beef brisket. Even if Madeline didn't want to see him, Holly was a foodie. She wouldn't pass on the meal. And Madeline loved Rosie's cooking. The three of them could have lunch. A nice *friend*ly gesture that would feed his heart right along with his belly. Plus, he would finally get to check out her storefront.

He quickly told his father his plans. Duke gave him a

thumbs-up. "I think I'll get a nap myself with Rosie after we eat. Take your time."

Forrest twisted his lips. He was going to take those words at face value.

On his way to Maddie's, Forrest second-guessed his lunch plans. Maybe he should have called to see if she was available before just showing up. She could be with clients. His hands gripped the wheel. He would keep going.

Madeline had to eat sometime.

What if she'd already eaten lunch? He scratched his head before snapping his fingers. *The invitation.* He could always say he was dropping by to accept the evite to the Fortune Family Day in person and check out her place. Feeble. But it was all he had. He didn't care how flimsy the reason, he just had to see her, to be in her presence, breathing the same air that she was.

He parked three rows away from the Let's Get the Party Started sign. The parking lot was almost full. A swell of pride formed in his chest at Madeline's tenacity. Starting over after a public scandal wasn't easy. Yet she had done so with dignity and aplomb. He was rooting for her success. However, he knew that even without his cheerleading, she was going to achieve it and then some.

Gathering the food, Forrest exited his truck, his chin held high.

Another man, parked in front of her business, jumped out of his customized sports car and swaggered—*yes, swaggered*—his way into Madeline's building.

The only reason Forrest noticed him was *that car* and the ginormous bouquet he held. Plus, there were three men creeping behind him, cameras in hand.

The guy wore ripped jeans and a punk denim vest.

Maybe he was famous? But Forrest couldn't identify him past those big sunglasses and baseball cap. He was taller and broader than he was, and Forrest wasn't a man of average height.

Forrest slowed. Dang, maybe he should have brought flowers. He shook off that sentiment. He wasn't a man who compared himself to others, and he wouldn't start now. Madeline would appreciate his gesture.

But still, who *was* that dude? A potential love interest? Madeline was a gorgeous woman, and he had rebuffed her multiple times. Maybe she had moved on already. He darted back to his truck, started up the engine and actually started to back out of the spot, when he slammed on the brakes.

Shoot, he was acting like he didn't know Madeline. He knew his friend well. She felt things deeply. Even if Bouquet Dude was shooting his shot—and Forrest couldn't blame the man for trying—there was no way Madeline would be open to meeting someone else already. As a matter of fact, Dude would probably need some comfort food after her beautiful letdown. Well, he had enough for four.

Chuckling, Forrest pulled forward into the spot. A horn honked. That's when he realized someone had been waiting to park. Forrest apologized, picked up the food and trekked toward her entrance. By this point, his tummy was growling. He was so ready to get his grub on.

Forrest pulled open the door. What he saw made his mouth drop. Because he had been *so wrong* about Dude. Dude was down on one knee, and Madeline was all smiles.

Chapter Fifteen

Amid the flashes of light, a man entered their shop holding the most gorgeous bouquet she had ever seen and shut the door behind him. She peeked at the insignia and saw that they had been designed by Emerald Ridge Floral. She loved that he had supported local businesses. The man drew the blinds before taking off his cap and sunglasses. "Hello, Evergreen."

Holly fluttered her lashes and looked down at her feet. "Hammer." They stared into each other's eyes, engaged in an intimate conversation without either saying a word. It was daggone hot to watch. She had also never seen her friend shy or tongue tied.

Madeline had to clear her throat to remind them of her presence. "If you'll excuse me, I'll give you two some privacy."

"No, don't go," Holly said, reaching over to take Madeline's hand in hers. "I need you here with me. I need a witness, so I know I'm not hallucinating like last time."

Dante took a step. "I've been looking for you, Holly Webster."

"And I have been looking for you, Dante Martinelli." Holly's chin quivered. "You left me." The raw vulnerability in her voice made Madeline tear up. She squeezed Holly's hand.

"I didn't want to," Dante said, waving a hand outside the door at the paparazzi. "I fell in love with you and only sought to spare you all that."

"It was my decision to make," Holly shot back, a little edge in her voice.

He nodded. "I know that now. The minute I left, I knew it was a big mistake to let you go. I should have followed my heart, but I didn't even know your name." Dante held out the bouquet. Holly released Madeline's hand and accepted the flowers. She sniffed before giving him a tender smile.

"These are lovely," she breathed.

"I wanted something that reflected my love for you," Dante replied, drawing Holly close.

Madeline moved to the furthest corner of the room. She should probably go into her office, but she was committed to watching how this all played out. And she was taking mental notes. This man was saying all the right words and he spoke with such certainty about his feelings that Madeline didn't doubt his veracity.

And this was only after one day. She marveled at that.

Dante got on one knee. Holly sucked in a breath.

Madeline was the proverbial fly on the wall as a fairy tale played out before her, complete with a happy ending. She couldn't stop smiling. For a brief moment, she wondered what this would mean for the patisserie she had just purchased, but then assured herself that things would work out as they should. Love was beautiful when it was reciprocated and not one-sided.

That's when the door opened and Forrest walked in,

holding a large bag of food. Madeline's eyes went wide, surprised to see him. She placed a finger over her mouth and beckoned him to be quiet.

"Holly, the day we spent together was more than enough for me to know that I want to spend the rest of my days making more discoveries with you." Madeline's eyes locked onto Forrest's. Dante took out a square-cut, yellow-diamond ring. "Will you marry me?"

Holly nodded, tears of joy brimming in her eyes. "Yes, I will."

Madeline cheered as Forrest congratulated them both and volunteered to take pictures. Then they had a celebratory lunch of the beef brisket and salad that Forrest had brought with him. Madeline gave him a quick tour after Holly and Dante disappeared into her office.

"So, what made you decide to come by today?" Madeline asked, even as her heart rate sped up at the sight of him.

"I missed you," Forrest said, moving into her personal space. "The girls, too. They have been asking for you nonstop." Aww. She could see Ivy and Violet's little brows furrowed, wondering where she was. He pointed to the leftover food. "So, I came with a peace offering."

"I wouldn't say that we were fighting. It felt more like an impasse to me."

"No, but we're at a standstill, and I need you to know how important you are to me."

"I know that," Madeline said. "This isn't about how we value each other. This is about taking things beyond friendship, beyond chemistry and attraction. You won't allow yourself to, when we have a chance at the real thing." She sighed heavily. "I just watched a stranger propose to my best friend—a woman he had known for only twenty-four hours. He dared to put his feelings on the line, and all I'm asking is for you to try to do the same."

Forrest looked like he was ready to bolt through the door. That pained her heart. She changed the subject. "I have plushies that I had made from self-portraits for your girls. If it's okay with you, I'll bring them over later."

"Sure. They will be ecstatic to see you." He took her hand. "Thanks for always thinking of them."

"Of course. I love them." She loved him, too, but bit back the words. Madeline was open with her emotions. Holding back took a *lot* out of her, but she wasn't going to set herself up for more heartache by uttering the words. *A reason or a season*, she reminded herself. Time would tell how this panned out.

"We all love you," he said.

Those words triggered her ire. Madeline spun to face him. "Is that the *best* that you can do?" He gazed at her with puppy dog eyes. "I'm sorry but that is a cop-out. You're braver than that. You just don't know it."

"You deserve more than what I have to give."

"You have everything I need, but you can't see that our bond is strong enough to sustain us. You don't want to take the chance, which is why I said we needed to take a step back. And dang it, I hate that I'm once again pleading with you, when I said I wouldn't anymore, but I don't know how to get you to see that our bond is strong enough to sustain us. It's like you're in this emotional rut and you're at a standstill."

Those words hung between them until a passerby walked in to ask her about her business. With a nod of her head, she realized that she might have to let him go and she wasn't just talking about now, so he could see to his girls.

Because Madeline didn't know how to be around him and his daughters and not fall further in love. Madeline didn't want to spend her life waiting, because she had a lot of love to give and she wanted a family of her own.

So when she went to Forrest's home, she would be saying goodbye. For good. Just as she pulled off, she received a call from her mother.

"Why wasn't I invited to the Fortune Family Day?" Taffy asked, her voice filling the vehicle. "I had to hear about this from a friend. I'm very much a Fortune."

"My siblings will be there, and I didn't want any drama. I know how you feel about them—"

"Were the other mothers invited?"

Madeline hated the hurt in her mother's tone. "Yes. I was trying to spare your feelings."

"Spare my…" Taffy inhaled. After a beat, she asked, "Madeline, are you ashamed of me?"

Sometimes. A little bit. But she couldn't tell her mother that. Madeline hunched her shoulders and tried to provide a delicate answer. "I don't know if I would use the word *ashamed* per se. I love you, but, Mom, you can be a bit much. And you always don't think about the consequences of your actions."

"What do you mean?"

"Mom, when you called that emergency meeting with the family, your only focus was on getting to Damaris. I saw the look on your face. You delighted in exposing her affair right in front of her son, my brother. You didn't think twice about how this might have affected Hayes.

He was shocked and hurt. He had to wonder if Dad was his father."

"Yeah, but Hayes forgave Damaris and the test results proved he was a Fortune," she sputtered. "So that all ended well. In fact, if it weren't for me, Damaris would always be wondering about the paternity."

"See, that's why it's hard for me to talk to you about things that matter to me, because when I do, you make excuses. You don't take responsibility for your actions."

"What do you want me to do? Apologize to Hayes?" From her mother's tone, Madeline could tell that Taffy found that suggestion ludicrous.

"Yes. That would be a start. It would be nice to see you think of others besides yourself. Even in the movies, the villain isn't a villain *all* the time. They have at least one redeemable quality that gives us a glimpse of their humanity." *Oy.* Madeline raked a hand through her hair. Her mouth got away from her.

Her mother sucked in a breath. "Ouch. That was harsh."

"Mom, I didn't mean that the way it came out." She blew out a long breath of air. "I was trying to make a point. I wasn't calling you a villain." Her stomach tensed while she waited for her mother's response.

To her surprise, Taffy chuckled. "I guess I deserved that. I know what you mean, honey. I know I can be catty, and it's true. I had no business snooping into Damaris's life, but I was focused on my own hurt. I saw myself as lashing out at Archibald—not anyone else—but you're right. I wasn't thinking about Hayes, and I should have been."

Madeline hit the brakes then looked in her rearview.

Thankfully, no one was behind her. "Hold up. Mom, are you actually *apologizing*? Hang on just a minute." She pulled over to a safe spot, so she could call her mother on FaceTime. When Taffy answered, she said, "Please tell me if you're owning up to your misdeeds, so I can record this, because this is monumental."

Taffy rolled her eyes. "Really, Madeline. You are so dramatic at times. You must have gotten that from Archibald because it couldn't be from me."

Madeline cracked up. "You're full of jokes today, Mom." Her heart was happy because she had never foreseen having such an open conversation with her mother and having her actually listen.

"Like you said, every villain has a redeemable quality." Tears formed in Taffy's eyes. "*You're* my redeemable quality, Madeline. You're the best of me."

She lost her breath. "Wow. What a beautiful thing to say." She dabbed at her eyes. Madeline wanted to ask if Taffy were sick or dying, why she was so free with her emotions, but Madeline didn't want to ruin the authenticity of the moment. Instead, she soaked in all of what her mom had to say.

"I'd be crushed if anyone hurt you the way I hurt Hayes." Taffy placed a hand over her chest. "I know I won't win any Mother of the Year awards, but I do love you with all my heart. I did care for your father in my own way, until that scum—" She coughed. "I do wish love and happiness for you." Her voice hitched. "I want you to find bliss with a man who deserves you."

Madeline fell apart then. She couldn't believe she was having this conversation with her mother on the side of the road, but if Taffy could put herself out there, then she could open up, too. She poured out everything to her mother about her relationship with Forrest.

Her mother listened, comforted, and didn't utter a disparaging word. Then she did something that further surprised Madeline. Taffy took her side. "I'm with you, dear. Stand your ground. Forrest sounds like a wonderful man, but he needs to make up his mind." But she was very much Taffy. "Because he can't expect to saddle you with a ready-made family and not put a ring on your finger or even say those three big words. Because telling someone you love them is no small thing."

Madeline burst out in laughter. "I love you, Mom. And please tell me you're coming this weekend. I could use a hug."

Taffy blew her a kiss. "You've got it, honey. I'll be there, but no slobbering, because I'm wearing designer to the cookout."

Since he knew Madeline was stopping by, Forrest had been on the lookout for her vehicle, which was why he was able to open the door for Cora as soon as she pulled into his driveway. She had texted that she and Dean were back from their trip and that she would be over to pick up Ivy and Violet that evening.

"Hey, I thought you weren't coming until at least another hour," Forrest said. He'd texted Junie to bring them downstairs.

"Traffic was lighter than expected so we made it in good time. How were the girls?"

"Great as usual. I took them swimming today at my parents' house. They had a ball."

"Aww. Please send me pictures. I'm going to sign them up for private swimming lessons this summer."

"I will."

She followed him inside. "May I go up and surprise them?"

"Actually, Junie is already bringing them down, so you can just wait here. They'll only be a minute or two." He gestured to the couch, and she took a seat. "I've been checking out pictures of the playground at the amusement park and it really would be an amazing venue for the girls' second birthday."

"Oh yes. I'll ask Madeline today since she's on her way over. Though she plans to buy the property from me, I don't think she'd have a problem. Actually, I'm pretty sure she won't."

Cora waggled her brows. "And, of course, she'll be invited."

Just then, Madeline rapped at the door. He hollered for her to enter. She walked inside, holding the plushies.

Cora jumped to her feet. "Oh, those are so cute." She strutted over to where Madeline stood to get a closer look. Forrest sat on the couch across from where Cora had been sitting while they'd spoken.

"I had them done from Ivy and Violet's artwork."

"I love that idea."

"Yeah, you can get custom plushies from a photo or your pet. I didn't know they would turn out this good though."

Both women fawned over the plushies made from his daughters' self-portraits. The way Madeline and Cora gushed over the artwork, you would think that Ivy and Violet were related to Van Gogh or some other famous artist.

Junie came down the stairs with the girls. She handed them over with a quick greeting, then left to finish cleaning their playroom.

"Mommy!" Ivy ran to Cora.

"Maddie!" Violet ran to Madeline and wrapped her arms around Madeline's legs.

That gave Forrest a jolt. The girls were treating Madeline the way they did Dean. Like a bonus parent. So was Cora.

"Forrest and I were just talking the twins second b-i-r-t-h day plans." She spelled out most of the word so the girls wouldn't know what they were talking about. "We would love to use the playground at the amusement park, if that's cool with you?"

Now, Forrest had wanted to be the one to ask Madeline about using the playground, but he wasn't about to say anything to Cora. He loved that his friend and the mother of his children were able to get along because of his daughters. He needed to try a little harder with Dean, especially since Ivy and Violet loved him.

"Oh, I love that idea." Madeline's eyes shone. "Of course you can use the playground."

"Good. I'll make sure Forrest updates you with the theme once we've decided what we're going to do."

"That sounds great. Thanks for including me," Madeline said. "I'm honored and I'd love to handle the decorations."

Just like that, Forrest had a flash of how his future with Madeline could play out. It wasn't terrifying, like he had envisioned. In fact, it was natural. Easy. Cora was treating Madeline like she was his significant other, and that felt right to him.

Cora gave him a pointed look, but Forrest had no clue what he was expected to say, so he nodded and smiled. Then he busied himself with playing with the girls, though he kept his ear cocked to listen in on the conversation.

"If you aren't doing anything this weekend, I'd love if you and your husband come to our Fortune Family Day at the amusement park."

"Oh, we would be *delighted*," Cora said. "Dean loves roller-coaster rides and he's been asking me to see if we could snag an invite to Kate's 100th birthday party."

Forrest shook his head. He hoped Madeline didn't feel manipulated, but judging from the smile on her face, she was thrilled. Both women were getting along like ducks in water, and a good rapport between the women would be essential if Madeline were a stepmother to the girls. Whoa. Where had that thought come from?

"Well, tell your hubby to consider himself invited. The more, the merrier. I'll get Forrest to send you the details," Madeline said. "Although he has yet to officially accept my invite."

"Of course I'm coming," Forrest told her.

Cora pulled out her phone. "Actually, let's eliminate the middle man. Here's my number."

Forrest clenched his jaw. Now *that* he disliked. But then, he considered that he and Dean did have each other's contact info. It might not be a big deal.

"Well, we'd better get going," Cora said, calling to Ivy and Violet. Both girls hugged him and then ran over to Madeline for hugs. The love on their faces for her made his breath hitch. He loved her, too.

It took some prying, but they were finally out the door. Forrest walked out with them to help get the girls into their car seats. Once the girls were buckled in, Cora held open the driver's door and gave him a piercing look. "That one's a keeper."

"I agree." He squared his shoulders and said something he never pictured he would say to his ex-wife. "I've fallen for her but I'm just afraid to go there. I don't want to make the same mistake twice."

Cora touched his chest. "It's because you're afraid that you *should* go there. Grab onto love with all you've got. Everything else will work itself out in time."

She was right. He needed to be grabbing onto Madeline instead of allowing her to slip out of his life.

Madeline came outside as Cora was driving off. "Do you have to go?" he asked.

"Yeah, I have a menu tasting at the hotel for Kate's birthday party." She glanced at her watch. "I have to be there in an hour, and I wanted to go home and change."

"Do you want company?" he asked. "We could get real fancy and make a fun date of it."

Her eyes flashed before she doused it. "I don't think that's a good idea. A date implies there's more between us and you've already made your position abundantly clear. Besides, I'm not just going to be eating—I'll be picking out the plating and the linens."

"I know what a date implies, which is why I suggested it. I know I'm asking a lot after being so indecisive, but I'm pleading for another chance."

She narrowed her eyes and fretted with her lower lip as she studied him. His heart thundered in his chest. Forrest thought Madeline was going to turn him down. But he breathed a sigh of relief when she lowered her lashes.

"I'll pick you up in forty-five minutes." She cocked her head. "Do you really want to get dolled up for a tasting?"

"It's not a tasting. It's a date."

"Alright. Well, the color theme is black and gold for Kate's one-hundredth so I suppose we wear those colors in tribute." There was a hint of excitement in her voice. A hint of hope, and that invigorated him.

"Yep, I got it. See you in a few." He rushed inside to dust off his black suit.

Chapter Sixteen

She had never washed and dried her hair so fast, but she was thankful that her tresses cooperated, leaving her with shiny, lustrous strands. Madeline put on light makeup and paused at her reflection. Why was she doing this? Putting herself out there once again, when Forrest could change his mind. Again. Because she loved him. Plain and simple. And Madeline didn't want to look back one day and wonder, what if. She donned a black gown and gold sandals. She also packed a small overnight bag just in case and rested it by her front door.

When she stepped outside her condo, Forrest was at her door with flowers.

"The flowers are lovely," she said. "Thank you."

"You look divine," he said. He was dressed in all black with gold cufflinks and a gold Patek Philippe. This man was bringing his A game. This was very much a *date* date. She placed the flowers inside and grabbed her overnight bag.

His eyes raked over her body like he was ravenous before he banked his passion, took her bag and held out his arm.

Madeline linked her arm in his, appreciating his firm grip because her legs were all wobbly and her lips trembled. Desire coursed through her veins, and she was tempted to suggest they skip the tasting. She was hungry for a different kind of meal.

However, Madeline would see how things played out with Forrest on their date before she decided how the night ended. In the meantime, though, she had a good-looking man by her side, a beautiful night, and an elegant all-you-can-eat buffet awaiting. She was going to enjoy herself tonight.

He led her toward a Bentley. “Your chariot awaits,” he said, ushering her inside. *Well, dang.* She hadn’t even known he owned one of these. She settled into the luxurious leather, closed her eyes and smiled. Forrest put her bag in the back.

They pulled up to the hotel, and he handed off the keys to the valet. Arm in arm, they made their way to the grand ballroom.

In the corner of the room were tables that featured several centerpieces, linen choices and table settings. The decorator had selected a few designs and now Madeline had to make the final decisions. Kate had given her free rein on this, and Madeline enjoyed having a loose budget. It left her with the option to be whimsical and extravagant just like Kate Fortune.

The only thing the old woman truly desired was for Susannah to show up. That was the one thing guaranteed to make Kate have a fun night. Madeline just hoped the reclusive celebrity would change her mind and make an appearance. She had posted information in the town paper, praying Susannah would read it.

“What’s on your mind?” Forrest asked, interjecting into her thoughts.

"I was just thinking about Susannah. I am trying to respect her request for privacy, but also meet Kate's wish for Susannah to attend her birthday party."

"That's a slippery slope. You'll be able to think better once you've eaten." He led her to the center of the room where a table set for two awaited them, adorned with a small centerpiece and a flickering candle. Two servers started them off with red wines and appetizers. Madeline was determined to try them all.

Forrest was just as adventurous. He pulled his chair next to hers, feeding her samples as they were presented. It was so erotic that Madeline literally groaned a few times when his fingertips grazed her lips.

They talked and laughed over dinner before she made all the final choices. Madeline couldn't recall a time she had had so much fun on a work gig.

"I don't want this night to end," she mused as they exited the hotel.

His voice dropped. "It doesn't have to. I'm up for whatever you want." Forrest's hand rested across her lower back as he whispered in her ear, "Just say the word."

Oh, she knew what she wanted. Madeline licked her lips. "Word."

Forrest rested Madeline on her back in the middle of his bed. He had just ditched his tux, tossing it on top of her dress. As lovely as she had looked in the dress, Madeline looked even better without it.

He padded across his carpet to turn on the fan.

"I'm not hot," she said.

"You will be."

"Oh." She covered her mouth with her hand and tittered. He smirked at the eager anticipation in that one word.

Using his mouth and hands, Forrest kindled Madeline's fire, loving all of her sounds. Once she was ready, he entered her glorious cavern and stilled. Pleasure washed over him.

"Man, I've missed you." Forrest gritted his teeth as his passions engulfed him.

"I've missed you too," she huffed out.

Gripping her tight, Forrest took her with him and, together, they rode the waves to completion.

"That was…whew," she exclaimed, her body glistened with sweat. "I don't have the words. All I can do is breathe."

Wrapped in each other's arms, Forrest stayed awake until her breathing evened out. Under the moonlight glow, he planted kisses on that creamy skin before snuggling her under his arms. He closed his eyes and surrendered to sleep, knowing there was nowhere else he wanted to be.

His cell buzzed in the wee hours of the morning. It was his mother calling, which was not a good sign. He popped up in bed. Hysterical, she told him that she had taken his father to the ER. Something about his father breathing heavy and clutching his chest.

Rosie stressed that they were running tests and that he didn't have to come. She would let him know what was going on, but Forrest wasn't having that. "I'm on my way."

He jumped out of bed and hauled on his clothes. He took a moment to count to three as his heart pounded in his chest. If something happened to his dad, he didn't know what he would do. Forrest turned to rouse Madeline to let her know that he had an emergency, the bed was empty.

Madeline was slipping into a pair of shorts and a tank top. “I'm coming with you.”

Together, they brushed their teeth at the his and her sinks in his master bath. Their teeth brushing, even more than the physical one that they had just shared, made him feel closer to her. A few minutes later, they dashed out the door.

Madeline headed to the driver's side of his truck. “I'll drive.” Forrest didn't argue. He had forgotten what it was like to have a partner with him. Someone to share his fears and to cover when he was shaky. Cora's words, *She's a keeper*, came back to him. Madeline Fortune definitely was.

Love for her flooded his heart. He squeezed her thigh and whispered, “I really appreciate you.”

She spared him a quick glance, her hands steady on the wheel. “You'd do the same for me.” Her faith in him caught him off guard, even though she spoke the truth.

Forrest settled in his seat, praying his mother hadn't downplayed what was going on with his father. At some point during the short trip, Madeline linked her fingers with his, and he was able to draw from her strength as he prayed for his father's strength.

She pulled up to the ER entrance. “Go on in. I'll go park and then meet you in there.”

“No. We'll go in together.”

She did as he wished. As soon as they parked and were out of the truck, Forrest hugged her, his grip tight. She rubbed his back. “He will be alright. I'm right here.”

“And what if he isn't?” Forrest dared to ask.

"I'll still be here."

Those words grounded him. He reached to take her hand in his, and, together, they rushed inside.

Hours later, just before daybreak, four people walked out of the emergency room joking and laughing. Relief mingled with gratitude as they released their fears to the wind.

"Who knew heartburn could feel like that?" Duke grumbled. "I've never felt such piercing chest pain in my life."

"It can be quite painful," Madeline said reassuringly.

"You gave me quite a scare." His mother tsked. "Starting today, you're back on your diet and I don't want to hear any fuss about it."

"After the night I had, bring on the salmon, the salad and the seltzer water. You won't hear a peep out of me."

Forrest chuckled. He gave his father a week before he was back to his ornery self. Seeing his mother give Duke the side-eye, he would guess she was thinking the same thing.

"What a way to start the weekend," Duke said with a yawn. "I'm not sure we'll make it to the Fortune Family Day today." Madeline had extended an invite to them while they'd waited for the lab results.

"Please, rest up. I'll have a courier drop off your meals."

"Thank you, dear," Rosie said. "We appreciate your thoughtfulness."

He and Madeline saw his parents off.

"I was afraid to hope," Forrest admitted gruffly.

She touched his cheek. "I get it. But hope wouldn't be

hope if you didn't have fear." She rubbed her eyes. "If you could drop me off at home, I'll get some much-needed z's before this afternoon." Forrest was glad the girls were with Cora, because he, too, could use a few hours of uninterrupted sleep.

"I don't want you to leave." He gave Madeline a tender kiss.

She quirked her lips. "Good thing my bed is big enough for both of us."

Chapter Seventeen

She couldn't have anticipated a better turnout for the Fortune Family Day. Madeline stood with Holly by the main booth, handing out mini tarts and eclairs with their promo materials as more people entered the park. So far, they had garnered significant interest in Holly's goodies.

As far as her eyes could see, Fortunes were enjoying the different rides at the amusement park along with the rest of the town. The smell of cotton candy, roasted nuts, pizza and barbecue permeated the compound, and the sounds of laughter brought joy to her heart.

Ultimately, this was what life was all about: spending quality time with the ones you loved and with those who loved you.

The press had already passed through to take pictures from their soft opening for their town paper. Now, at her request, they were on the rides or stuffing their faces with some of the best food Emerald Ridge had to offer.

The temperature was in the upper nineties, so Madeline and Holly had set up in a shack, running the air conditioner with a generator.

While they served others, she provided her bestie with the scintillating update of her unexpected night with Forrest. Holly had already shared that Dante had taken the red-eye to a photo shoot. They had been holed up in his hotel room for the past two days.

"So, did Forrest tell you that he loved you yet?" Holly asked once there was a lull in the queue. "That's the only thing that's missing from this juicy accounting."

"No."

"Did you tell him how you felt then?"

"No, I didn't. I'm playing it cool. Plus, we were too busy doing other stuff for any declarations." Her toes curled every time she thought about their hot night together. She was pretty sure she had lost a good pound or two through sweat.

Holly flapped her arms. "Chicken."

"What? I will not be the one to say it first," she sputtered.

"Why not?"

"You think I want it known that I said *I love you* first? Not after all this up and down between us."

"Girl, that's lame. As long as Forrest knows how you feel, that's all that matters."

"He knows," Madeline insisted, popping a tart inside her mouth. "Just like I know how he feels about me. We don't need the words." Her heart ached to hear them though. She had almost blurted them out this morning before he'd left her house to tend to his ranch, but she had held back.

"I get that," Holly said. "But Forrest doesn't strike me as a man who can be easily swayed. That man isn't going to do or say anything that he doesn't want to."

Madeline couldn't deny that truth. Shoot, Holly was right. She glanced at her friend with exasperation. "Thanks for bursting my happy balloon. Now you have me questioning why he hasn't said the words." Doubt lined her gut, souring her good mood. He had asked for a second chance, but a second chance meant what exactly. This whole back and forth was annoying as ever.

"I didn't mean to puncture your confidence… I just don't want you to be complacent. You deserve better than to settle for anything less than love."

Some teens approached, and Holly went to cater to them. Madeline spotted her mother strutting her way. Taffy was dressed in a silk blouse, white cropped-leg pants and a pair of heels. She had a straw hat and a large pair of shades. "Mom, you made it!" she yelled out.

Taffy held on to her hat and stepped inside. "Thank goodness for AC. It's hotter than hades out there. I don't think I'll get this dust out of my shoes."

"I told you to wear sneakers and to lose the makeup in this heat."

"I could never." She touched her chest, sounding scandalized. "The other wives are sure to be dressed like supermodels. I've got to represent." Taffy threw Holly air kisses.

Madeline rolled her eyes. "They're not checking for you."

"Quit doing that with your eyes before they get stuck." She held out her arms. "Well, come get the hug I promised you." There was a hint of vulnerability in her tone.

Madeline embraced her mother, inhaling the scent of her Valentino perfume. She closed her eyes as she rested her head against her mother's bosom. There was no place like her mother's arms.

Taffy tapped her on the shoulders. "You're going to break my back if you don't let up."

She snorted and tightened her hold before releasing her mom. Though Taffy fussed with her about it, Madeline could see she was pleased.

Brushing at her blouse, her mom asked, "So where is this man who got my baby all twisted up?"

"That's an apt phrase," Holly snickered.

Taffy's head snapped back. "Wait, has there been a new development?"

"Let me fill you in," Holly said, leading her mother to the other end of the shack. A calculated move because Madeline saw Forrest coming her way. The way that T-shirt stretched across his chest and the way those jeans hung on his hips could only be described as hot. Holly had just spared him an inquisition.

Forrest had been at the ranch since this morning, but they had been exchanging raunchy texts. She was sure that it had been her last suggestive proposition that had brought him here. A few heads turned to check him out, and Madeline puffed her chest. He only had eyes for her.

She hurried to meet him and tugged him toward the Ferris wheel. Forrest stopped behind a tent, snatching her close. Shielding them with his Stetson, he kissed her like they were the only ones in the park.

"I've been dying to do that all morning," he growled.

"Same," she breathed, pulling away. "Are your children here yet?"

"Yes, I think they are with Cora and Dean at the playground."

"Oh, cool. I can't wait to see them."

He nuzzled her ear. "I want a repeat of yesterday."

"Easy now, Cowboy. Good things come to those who

wait." She looked at her watch. "Oh, it's almost time. We'll do the Ferris wheel later when the park closes."

"I like the sound of that," he said. Then paused. "Wait. Time for what?"

"You'll see." Hand in hand, they strolled over to the toddler playground. Ivy and Violet ran to them with their arms open. Madeline waved at Cora and Dean, then made sure to hug both girls. They played with the twins for a bit before Madeline marched him to the front of the playground.

The construction workers were in the process of putting up a special banner that read, Happy 100th Birthday, Kate Fortune. It had been painted in gold and black, the colors to celebrate her centennial party.

He placed a hand on his hip. "Wow. Seeing that makes it all real. Kate is going to be a hundred years old. She has lived through decades of presidents, wars and technological advances, and she isn't showing signs of slowing down anytime soon. Heck, millions of people haven't lived that long."

"Yes, what's wonderful is she can look back and say that she has loved, she has lived, and she has touched many lives." Madeline cocked her head. "How many of us can say the same?"

The vision of that banner stayed with him. A century was a remarkable feat. He marveled at that for a few days.

If Forrest lived to be a hundred, he didn't want to look back on his life and not have Madeline by his side because of his unwarranted fears and hard head. Yes, she would always be his true friend, but he needed her on a deeper, permanent level. And so did his daughters.

Madeline needed to know exactly how much she meant to him. To do so, Forrest had crafted the perfect plan of how to make it right. And after a busy few days, he had everything in place. Now, it was time to execute.

He sent Madeline a text.

Let's go for a ride later today.

Which kind?

Ha! Temperance and Samson could use the exercise.

What time?

6:30 p.m. Come stay the night.

She sent a thumbs-up emoji. He clenched his jaw. Except for when they were under the sheets, Madeline kept their conversation super casual. But hopefully that would all change tonight.

Madeline pulled in next to Forrest's truck by the barn. It was a perfect May night. The temperature was mild, and there was a light wisp of a breeze. She went into the barn. Forrest was already there, brushing down Temperance. The sight of him made her breath catch. She didn't know it was possible to fall deeper in love, but every time she was in his presence, that was what happened.

She wanted this man in her life for a lifetime. The question was, did he feel the same?

Her boots crunched across the hay. Forrest's head popped up. "Hey, you're here."

"My meeting ended earlier than I thought."

"No worries." He scooted next to her and gave her a searing kiss. "Are you ready?"

"Born ready."

She mounted Temperance. Forrest used the stirrups to sit astride Samson. Both horses went into a trot.

Madeline inquired about the girls.

"They're good—they are with Cora. I swear, I think they grew an inch since yesterday. I spoke to them today and they asked about you, as usual." He smiled. "From the day they met you, my daughters knew you were special. Do you know that children are a good judge of character?"

"No, I didn't know that."

"Yeah. If a child doesn't like you, that's not a good sign." He gave her a look of tenderness. "Ivy and Violet love you something fierce. You know that?"

Her cheeks warmed, and there was a slight hitch in her voice. "Yes, I do. I love them just as much if not more."

Forrest's brow furrowed.

"Are you alright?"

"Yeah. Just thinking about how I was too hardheaded to see what my daughters were showing all along."

Before she could process what he meant, Forrest urged Samson forward.

"Gallop," he commanded. The horse instantly picked up speed. He gestured for her to follow. "Let's ride. We have a ways to go."

"You heard him, girl." Madeline used her heel and tapped Temperance. "Let's pick up the pace." It was like her horse had been waiting for her cue. She shot past Forrest and Samson, then neighed. Madeline laughed. It was like she was challenging Samson. Well, of course, they weren't about to be bested. What ensued was a race between the horses and a lot of fun and laughter with their owners.

Eventually, she allowed Forrest to move ahead.

He joked, "I won."

"Only because you know where we're headed." She took in her surroundings. She had no idea where they were. "Where are we going, by the way?"

He pointed. "Just around the bend. Behind those trees."

The minute they cleared the bushes, she gasped. "The shed. Oh my goodness, this was where I found shelter."

He dismounted and helped her off hers.

"The very same. It was so far onto my property that I forgot about it." He pierced her with those brown eyes. "I missed it, even though it was right there, under my nose." That made her blush. He jutted his chin. "However, as you see, the shed has been upgraded."

The rickety shed had been replaced with a newer, larger one. "When did you do this?"

"Three days ago." Another look. "I was motivated to move fast."

There was a special overhang big enough to secure the horses and protect them from the elements. They secured their reins to the doorpost.

Then Forrest jogged up the three steps and unlocked the door using a smart code. He recited the four-digit number twice and even had her repeat it. "We're the only two people with this code. Do you recognize it?"

"No."

"It's the day we met."

Her mouth formed an *O*. "It is..." Gosh, this man was so thoughtful.

His voice dropped. "This is our spot. Our oasis."

Our. Madeline's tummy fluttered and her heart galloped—maybe even faster than Samson and Temperance. Today was about more than a ride.

He pushed the door open and gestured for her to walk in ahead. She sucked in a breath. There was a king-sized bed built in there. And AC, which she appreciated. "How on earth did you fit that in here?"

Forrest chuckled. "Skillful engineering and design."

There was also a small stove, a mini refrigerator, and a shower. It could only hold one person at a time. Forrest smirked. "It was either the shower or the bed. You see where my priorities lie."

"I love it," she declared, hopping onto the bed. She peered up at him from under her lashes. "Do you want to try it out?"

"Do I ever." Forrest sat next to her and cupped her head, drawing her in for a long, lazy kiss. A slow burn. And, boy, was she heated. Forrest pulled away, looked at his watch and groaned. "We're out of time." He slapped his forehead. "I miscalculated. I didn't factor in that we would want to spend more time here right now."

She scrunched her nose. "Out of time for what?"

He stood and took her hand. "You'll see."

He held out a hand, but Madeline had other plans. Using the element of surprise, she tugged him down next to her and straddled him. Then she proceeded to kiss him with all the passion she could muster. Forrest was a goner.

Then his phone rang. He froze. "I've got to take this."

"Where are you guys?" a voice she thought she recognized as Holly's asked, but Forrest nestled his phone to his ear. "We got caught up… We'll be there." He disconnected and then stood. "As you could hear, we've got to go."

"Alright." He helped her stand, then strode over to the closet and took out a white eyelet dress. "You have to put this on. There is a washcloth and some of your favorite feminine essentials in the bathroom." Madeline didn't bother to question him. She just did as he asked, since she deduced that he had some surprise planned and she didn't want to ruin it. When she saw her favorite perfume, lingerie and all that, she laughed. Holly was definitely included in Forrest's plan.

There was a note in Forrest's handwriting. *Wear your hair loose.*

Once she was dressed, they exited their love shack.

Together, they walked about a half mile up the gravel path and then onto the grass before he stopped.

To her left was a field of flowers, and to her right was a hill. "It's gorgeous."

He smiled. "I had to pick the perfect location." He took her hand in his. She thought she saw a flash, but maybe it was the sun playing tricks on her. "Madeline, from the moment I met you, I knew you were something else. I just didn't know *what*." Forrest projected his voice, which was odd, considering they were alone out here, and his words didn't make sense. But she told herself to listen, be quiet, be patient. Maybe he was nervous.

"I knew you were a smart woman, a feisty woman, a caring woman, but I still had no clue who you were." He ran his fingers through her hair. "It took some time, but now I know that you are my person. My friend. My partner. My lover. And today, I hope to add one more thing to the list. My wife." Forrest dropped to one knee. Shock ran through her body. He took her hand and pulled out a gorgeous solitaire. Tears trekked down her face. "Madeline Fortune, I love you with all my heart. If I live to be a hundred, you're the one I want by my side. Will you do me the honor of being my wife and a bonus mom to my daughters?"

Blinded by her tears—*happy tears*—all she could do was nod. Forrest slipped the ring on her finger and then drew her in for a kiss. All too soon, he pulled away and yelled at the top of his lungs, "She said yes, y'all!"

Madeline shook her head. "Y'all?"

He tilted his head. "Take a look." She followed his gaze to the hills and gasped. There stood her mother, his parents, her siblings, Holly, Dante, Cora, Dean and the girls. There was even a photographer on the side capturing their moment. So, she hadn't imagined the flash. Each of them held on to a large banner that said, 100 Years Is Not Enough.

Lord, Madeline didn't want to ugly cry, but there was no holding back then, and it would all be on camera. There was a big whoop before their family and friends descended. A lot of cheering, congratulating and well-wishing ensued. Eventually, Madeline pulled Forrest aside. She had accepted his proposal but had yet to utter the words of her heart.

"What's wrong?" he asked.

"Nothing's wrong," she said, snuggling in his arms and touching his cheek. "Everything is one hundred percent right." She whispered, "Forrest Porter, I love you. I love you today. I'll love you tomorrow. And if I live long enough, I'll love you for the next hundred years."

Epilogue

April 10th
The 100th day, the following year

Some people might say that they had gotten carried away with their wedding theme, which was, simply, 100, but that number meant a lot to Madeline and Forrest. So, on the hundredth day, the following year, they recited their vows.

There were 100 guests in attendance, which had been no easy feat, considering how large their families were. Her bouquet had been designed using exactly 100 flowers, and there would be a keepsake of 100 different hand-chosen items for their wedding guests to commemorate their special day.

For their venue, they had opted to get married at the place where it all began, the amusement park. It had been closed for the day and a tent had been set up in the middle of the grounds.

It was now ten minutes to 1:00 p.m.

"Are you ready?" Holly asked, entering the trailer that Madeline had set up just outside the park. Her matron of honor was dressed in a champagne-colored gown customized for her baby bump. Forrest had asked his father to be his best man, and Jonathan and Trevor would serve as his groomsmen. Shelby and Jillian would be her bridesmaids.

"Oh, yes." With all the bustle around her that morning, Madeline had been oddly calm. Maybe it was because she had no doubt that she was with the man who was meant to be hers for the rest of her life. Or maybe she had to be since Taffy was being a motherzilla-of-the-bride. "I've been waiting for my mother. She's been complaining about her makeup and her hair." Madeline shook her head. "Nothing was right for her this morning. I'm so glad I made sure she had her own trailer, because she is just too much."

Holly giggled. "You would think she was the bride."

"Listen, after the way she was acting, even I think my mother *is* the bride."

"Let's get going. Forrest wants us to begin on time. He's been standing at that altar since twelve thirty."

Madeline smoothed her gown. "Is Penn ready?"

"Yes, he's right outside." She had chosen Penn to give her away, and their brother Hayes had agreed to escort Taffy down the aisle. "What about the twins?"

"They are with Forrest. Wait until you see them. They are the most adorable flower girls you'll ever see."

Madeline opened her mouth to ask another question, but Holly lifted a hand to stop her. "Yours truly was well trained. Everything is as it should be. Perfect. Now, let's get this show on the road."

"It took some doing but I couldn't quite get my vows to be exactly 100 words." Madeline fretted. Both she and Forrest had decided to write their own vows. "I really should have used Chat GPT."

"It's alright. I don't think Forrest is actually going to

count." Holly shooed her out of the trailer and onto the golf cart. "What matters to him is that he is marrying the woman of his dreams."

Taffy came out of her trailer wearing a champagne dress suitable for the mother of the bride and a stylish champagne hat, like royalty. Madeline breathed a sigh of relief. Her mother had begged Madeline to let her wear a floor-length gown, sending her three designs to choose from.

"I told you I'd get her in line," Holly said.

"If you weren't my partner, I'd give you a raise," Madeline told her.

Penn stood waiting for her. "Are you ready to go, sis?"

She slipped her arm through his. "One hundred percent ready."

Forrest stood at the altar amazed at the vision before him. Madeline's flowing red hair, her hand-sewn gown, which she told him featured 100 diamonds, made her appear almost ethereal. He could barely keep his eyes off her and kept touching her hair, her arms, to assure himself that this was finally happening. Waiting a hundred days felt like forever.

He couldn't wait for the part where he could kiss her senseless and whisk her away to their love shack.

The officiant cleared his throat. "I was told that Madeline and Forrest have prepared their vows."

Forrest pulled out his paper from his tux. "Madeline Fortune—" He addressed the crowd briefly, "That's two words down." Everyone chuckled. "—The number 100 signifies completion. You complete me in more ways than I can count. But I'm going to try. I give 100 percent of my heart. I wish for us to have 100 dreams answered, 100 memories of love, 100 laughters to share, 100 children—" The crowd cackled as her eyes went wide. He continued. "I will love you for a 100 lifetimes, and I will tell you that I love you 100 times, no more, no less." Madeline giggled. "My love for you is *infinite*. I can't put a number on how much you mean to me. But I can love you with all of my being, and even then it wouldn't be enough of the love you deserve."

Her eyes filled. He wiped her tears. "That's a little more than 100 words. Sorry."

"It's perfect," she sniffled and handed Holly her bouquet. Holly slipped Madeline her note.

"I tried to think of 100 ways to tell you that I love you, but I know it's best to show you." She licked her lips. "I promise to be the best bonus mom I can be to Ivy and Violet. I promise to listen when you need a friend. I promise to be your rock when life gets shaky. I promise to encourage you when you need my support. I will help you achieve your dreams, and I'll be by your side through all the ups and downs. Life can be a roller coaster, but it is worth living with you. I love you, Forrest. For always."

* * * * *